THE ORIGINAL SIN MURDERS

Volume 11: Zen and the Art of Investigation

A N T H O N Y   W O L F F

authorHOUSE®

AuthorHouse™
1663 Liberty Drive
Bloomington, IN 47403
www.authorhouse.com
Phone: 1-800-839-8640

*This is a work of fiction. All of the characters, names, incidents, organizations, and dialogue
in this novel are either the products of the author's imagination or are used fictitiously.*

Published by AuthorHouse 6/17/2014

ISBN: 978-1-4969-1820-8 (sc)
ISBN: 978-1-4969-1819-2 (e)

PREFACE

WHO ARE THESE DETECTIVES ANYWAY?

"The eye cannot see itself" an old Zen adage informs us. The Private I's in these case files count on the truth of that statement. People may be self-concerned, but they are rarely self-aware.

In courts of law, guilt or innocence often depends upon its presentation. Juries do not - indeed, they may not - investigate any evidence in order to test its veracity. No, they are obliged to evaluate only what they are shown. Private Investigators, on the other hand, are obliged to look beneath surfaces and to prove to their satisfaction - not the court's - whether or not what appears to be true is actually true. The Private I must have a penetrating eye.

Intuition is a spiritual gift and this, no doubt, is why *Wagner & Tilson, Private Investigators* does its work so well.

At first glance the little group of P.I.s who solve these often baffling cases seem different from what we (having become familiar with video Dicks) consider "sleuths." They have no oddball sidekicks. They are not alcoholics. They get along well with cops.

George Wagner is the only one who was trained for the job. He obtained a degree in criminology from Temple University in Philadelphia and did exemplary work as a investigator with the Philadelphia Police. These were his golden years. He skied; he danced; he played tennis; he had a Porche, a Labrador retriever, and a small sailboat. He got married and had a wife, two toddlers, and a house. He was handsome and well built, and he had great hair.

And then one night, in 1999, he and his partner walked into an ambush. His partner was killed and George was shot in the left knee and in his right shoulder's brachial plexus. The pain resulting from his injuries and the twenty-two surgeries he endured throughout the year that followed, left him addicted to a nearly constant morphine drip. By the time he was admitted to a rehab center in Southern California for treatment of his morphine addiction and for physical therapy, he had lost everything previously mentioned except his house, his handsome face, and his great hair.

His wife, tired of visiting a semi-conscious man, divorced him and married a man who had more than enough money to make child support payments unnecessary and, since he was the jealous type, undesirable. They moved far away, and despite the calls George placed and the money and gifts he sent, they soon tended to regard him as non-existent. His wife did have an orchid collection which she boarded with a plant nursery, paying for the plants' care until he was able to accept them. He gave his brother his car, his tennis racquets, his skis, and his sailboat.

At the age of thirty-four he was officially disabled, his right arm and hand had begun to wither slightly from limited use, a frequent result of a severe injury to that nerve center. His knee, too, was troublesome. He could not hold it in a bent position for an extended period of time; and when the weather was bad or he had been standing for too long, he limped a little.

George gave considerable thought to the "disease" of romantic love and decided that he had acquired an immunity to it. He would never again be vulnerable to its delirium. He did not realize that the gods of love regard such pronouncements as hubris of the worst kind and, as such, never allow it to go unpunished. George learned this lesson while working on the case, *The Monja Blanca*. A sweet girl, half his age and nearly half his weight, would fell him, as he put it, "as young David slew the big dumb Goliath." He understood that while he had no future with her, his future would be filled with her for as long as he had a mind that could think. She had been the victim of the most vicious swindlers he had ever encountered. They had successfully fled the country, but not the range of George's determination to apprehend them. These were master criminals, four of them, and he secretly vowed that he would make them fall, one by one. This was a serious quest. There was nothing quixotic about George Roberts Wagner.

While he was in the hospital receiving treatment for those fateful gunshot wounds, he met Beryl Tilson.

Beryl, a widow whose son Jack was then eleven years old, was working her way through college as a nurse's aid when she tended George. She had met him previously when he delivered a lecture on the curious differences between aggravated assault and attempted murder, a not uninteresting topic. During the year she tended him, they became friendly enough for him to communicate with her during the year he was in rehab. When he returned to Philadelphia, she picked him up at the airport, drove him home - to a house he had not been inside for two years - and helped him to get settled into a routine with the house and the botanical spoils of his divorce.

After receiving her degree in the Liberal Arts, Beryl tried to find a job with hours that would permit her to be home when her son came home from school each day. Her quest was daunting. Not only was a degree in Liberal Arts regarded as a 'negative' when considering an applicant's qualifications, (the choice of study having demonstrated a lack of foresight for eventual entry into the commercial job market) but by stipulating that she needed to be home no later than 3:30 p.m. each day, she further discouraged personnel managers from putting out their company's welcome mat. The supply of available jobs was somewhat limited.

Beryl, a Zen Buddhist and karate practitioner, was still doing part-time work when George proposed that they open a private investigation agency. Originally he had thought she would function as a "girl friday" office manager; but when he witnessed her abilities in the martial arts, which, at that time, far exceeded his, he agreed that she should function as a 50-50 partner in the agency, and he helped her through the licensing procedure. She quickly became an excellent marksman on the gun range. As a Christmas gift he gave her a Beretta to use alternately with her Colt semi-automatic.

The Zen temple she attended was located on Germantown Avenue in a two storey, store-front row of small businesses. Wagner & Tilson, Private Investigators needed a home. Beryl noticed that a building in the same row was advertised for sale. She told George who liked it, bought it, and let Beryl and her son move into the second floor as their residence. Problem solved.

While George considered himself a man's man, Beryl did not see herself as a woman's woman. She had no female friends her own age. None. Acquaintances, yes. She enjoyed warm relationships with a few older women. But Beryl, it surprised her to realize, was a man's woman. She liked men, their freedom to move, to create, to discover, and that inexplicable wildness that came with their physical presence and strength. All of her senses found them agreeable; but she had no desire to domesticate one. Going to sleep with one was nice. But waking up with one of them in her bed? No. No. No. Dawn had an alchemical effect on her sensibilities. "Colors seen by candlelight do not look the same by day," said Elizabeth Barrett Browning, to which Beryl replied, "Amen."

She would find no occasion to alter her orisons until, in the course of solving a missing person's case that involved sexual slavery in a South American rainforest, a case called *Skyspirit*, she met the Surinamese Southern District's chief criminal investigator. Dawn became conducive to romance. But, as we all know, the odds are always against the success of long distance love affairs. To be stuck in one continent and love a man who is stuck in another holds as much promise for high romance as falling in love with Dorian Gray. In her professional life, she was tough but fair. In matters of lethality, she preferred *dim mak* points to bullets, the latter being awfully messy.

Perhaps the most unusual of the three detectives is Sensei Percy Wong. The reader may find it useful to know a bit more about his background.

Sensei, Beryl's karate master, left his dojo to go to Taiwan to become a fully ordained Zen Buddhist priest in the Ummon or Yun Men lineage in which he was given the Dharma name Shi Yao Feng. After studying advanced martial arts in both Taiwan and China, he returned to the U.S.

to teach karate again and to open a small Zen Buddhist temple - the temple that was down the street from the office *Wagner & Tilson* would eventually open.

Sensei was quickly considered a great martial arts' master not because, as he explains, "I am good at karate, but because I am better at advertising it." He was of Chinese descent and had been ordained in China, and since China's Chan Buddhism and Gung Fu stand in polite rivalry to Japan's Zen Buddhism and Karate, it was most peculiar to find a priest in China's Yun Men lineage who followed the Japanese Zen liturgy and the martial arts discipline of Karate.

It was only natural that Sensei Percy Wong's Japanese associates proclaimed that his preferences were based on merit, and in fairness to them, he did not care to disabuse them of this notion. In truth, it was Sensei's childhood rebellion against his tyrannical faux-Confucian father that caused him to gravitate to the Japanese forms. Though both of his parents had emigrated from China, his father decried western civilization even as he grew rich exploiting its freedoms and commercial opportunities. With draconian finesse he imposed upon his family the cultural values of the country from which he had fled for his life. He seriously believed that while the rest of the world's population might have come out of Africa, Chinese men came out of heaven. He did not know or care where Chinese women originated so long as they kept their proper place as slaves.

His mother, however, marveled at American diversity and refused to speak Chinese to her children, believing, as she did, in the old fashioned idea that it is wise to speak the language of the country in which one claims citizenship.

At every turn the dear lady outsmarted her obsessively sinophilic husband. Forced to serve rice at every meal along with other mysterious creatures obtained in Cantonese Chinatown, she purchased two Shar Peis that, being from Macau, were given free rein of the dining room. These dogs, despite their pre-Qin dynasty lineage, lacked a discerning palate and proved to be gluttons for bowls of fluffy white stuff. When her husband retreated to his rooms, she served omelettes and Cheerios, milk instead of tea, and at dinner, when he was not there at all, spaghetti instead of chow mein. The family home was crammed with gaudy enameled furniture and torturously carved teak; but on top of the lion-head-ball-claw-legged coffee table, she always placed a book which illustrated the elegant simplicity of such furniture designers as Marcel Breuer; Eileen Gray; Charles Eames; and American Shakers. Sensei adored her; and loved to hear her relate how, when his father ordered her to give their firstborn son a Chinese name; she secretly asked the clerk to record indelibly the name "Percy" which she mistakenly thought was a very American name. To Sensei, if she had named him Abraham Lincoln Wong, she could not have given him a more Yankee handle.

Preferring the cuisines of Italy and Mexico, Sensei avoided Chinese food and prided himself on not knowing a word of Chinese. He balanced this ignorance by an inability to understand Japanese and, because of its inaccessibility, he did not eat Japanese food.

The Man of Zen who practices Karate obviously is the adventurous type; and Sensei, staying true to type, enjoyed participating in Beryl's and George's investigations. It required little time for him to become a one-third partner of the team. He called himself, "the ampersand in *Wagner & Tilson*."

Sensei Wong may have been better at advertising karate than at performing it, but this merely says that he was a superb huckster for the discipline. In college he had studied civil engineering; but he also was on the fencing team and he regularly practiced gymnastics. He had learned yoga and ancient forms of meditation from his mother. He attained Zen's vaunted transcendental states; which he could access 'on the mat.' It was not surprising that when he began to learn karate he was already half-accomplished. After he won a few minor championships he attracted the attention of several martial arts publications that found his "unprecedented" switchings newsworthy. They imparted to him a "great master" cachet, and perpetuated it to the delight of dojo owners and martial arts shopkeepers. He did win many championships and, through unpaid endorsements and political propaganda, inspired the sale of Japanese weapons, including nunchaku and shuriken which he did not actually use.

Although his Order was strongly given to celibacy, enough wiggle room remained for the priest who found it expedient to marry or dally. Yet, having reached his mid-forties unattached, he regarded it as 'unlikely' that he would ever be romantically welded to a female, and as 'impossible' that he would be bonded to a citizen and custom's agent of the People's Republic of China - whose Gung Fu abilities challenged him and who would strike terror in his heart especially when she wore Manolo Blahnik red spike heels. Such combat, he insisted, was patently unfair, but he prayed that Providence would not level the playing field. He met his femme fatale while working on *A Case of Virga*.

Later in their association Sensei would take under his spiritual wing a young Thai monk who had a degree in computer science and a flair for acting. Akara Chatree, to whom Sensei's master in Taiwan would give the name Shi Yao Xin, loved Shakespeare; but his father - who came from one of Thailand's many noble families - regarded his son's desire to become an actor as we would regard our son's desire to become a hit man. Akara's brothers were all businessmen and professionals; and as the old patriarch lay dying, he exacted a promise from his tall 'matinee-idol' son that he would never tread upon the flooring of a stage. The old man had asked for nothing else, and since he bequeathed a rather large sum of money to his young son, Akara had to content himself with critiquing the performances of actors who were less filially constrained than he. As far as romance is concerned, he had not thought too much about it until he worked on *A Case of Industrial Espionage*. That case took him to Bermuda, and what can a young hero do when he is captivated by a pretty girl who can recite Portia's lines with crystalline insight while lying beside him on a white beach near a blue ocean?

But his story will keep...

SUNDAY, JUNE 3, 2012

There was a time that George Wagner would have been honored and delighted to be invited to Sunday Dinner at The Hollyoak, the Eckersley's mansion. But now when he was invited he made sure that he ate elsewhere before he arrived at the great house on Philadelphia's Main Line. Although he frequently went to The Hollyoak on Sundays, he no longer wanted to dine there. Nobody did.

In recent months, the Sunday Dinner invitations had increased alarmingly. Old Lionel Eckersley had taken an interest in George's orchid collection which was housed in The Hollyoak's greenhouse, and he would drive with his wife, Alicia, from their in-town residence, a brownstone on Rittenhouse Square, to the estate on weekends to putter around the cattleya and phalaenopsis and ask George to reveal some of the more arcane tidbits about the private lives of tropical exotics.

It was not a single event that had precipitated the deluge of Sunday Dinner invitations now inflicted upon George. First, Alicia Eckersley's omniscient cook went to Vermont to raise her grandchildren while her daughter recovered from a compound leg fracture. Cookless, Alicia ceased to accept dinner invitations which she could not reciprocate. This gave her more time to watch movies on her DVD. And in this narrow window of opportunity, Alicia began to watch Al Pacino's *Richard III* and developed a suspicious interest in both. She announced that she was going to take a course in cooking, a decision that Lionel found commendable at the time. He had not realized the depth of Al's effect upon Alicia and was therefore stunned to discover that she had taken what he described as, "The most incomprehensible thing known to man": a course in traditional English cuisine.

1

Alicia had decided that having an ancestor who signed the Declaration of Independence gave her a mystical connection to a place named "Yorktown," and she understood Al's Winter of Discontent. Things about York began to obsess her. In particular, Yorkshire Pudding.

Two great galaxies collided in Lionel's firmament: a sexy Italian guy who had something to do with Yorkshire Pudding, and his wife's determination to master English cuisine.

Alicia had gone to Vassar and she had been a debutante. But her husband who was similarly divinely bred (by American standards) and who was regarded as a fine officer in the field in Viet Nam and then as the perfect example of an astute Philadelphia lawyer, a man of refinement and taste who was never given to vulgarity, began to be moved nightly to announce, "Alicia, you don't know your ass from a hole in the ground when it comes to cooking. Call a goddamned employment agency and get somebody in here who knows what the hell she's doing!" She refused.

And so it became obligatory for Lionel; his grandson Groff; any of Groff's friends who could be bribed; Beryl, when she had run out of excuses; her son Jack who liked to play shuffleboard with Groff at a nearby pub and was willing to pay for the pleasure by sitting at Alicia's dining table; and Sensei who regarded the challenge of eating her English cooking as a Zen exercise in Forbearance, to gather at The Hollyoak at precisely one o'clock on Sunday afternoon and like a jury deliberating a capital case sit around the large mahogany dining room table that had been set with Havilland porcelain, Waterford crystal and Gorham silverware.

Alicia Eckersley, too frail to lift the large pots and pans required to prepare food sufficient for a group of diners, restricted her efforts to directing a staff of three ladies who, she thought, knew something about cooking. In fact, they did not. This may be unfair since one was a native of Bangkok, another a native of Oaxaca, and the third, a lady born and raised in Baton Rouge. Alicia, unfortunately, was so bereft of culinary knowledge that she was unable to judge the veracity of any of their claims of skill or to mediate their loud and cryptic disputes. They argued constantly.

On Sunday, June 3rd, 2012, George Wagner and the rest of the anxious group assembled and prepared themselves to hear Alicia's dreaded pronouncement: "Today we are having a dinner that Richard II and Richard III of England both enjoyed.

"We shall begin with Yorkshire Pudding, go on to roast lamb with gravy, cheddar cheese and Stottle Cake; freshwater eel served with herb sauce, and for dessert, a suet pudding called Spotted Dick."

George could feel his arteries harden as she picked up a dinner bell. It tinkled, and the three kitchen ladies carried in the various dishes. Alicia, herself, had set the table and George and Lionel had made the orchid centerpiece which, all those assembled agreed, was more appetizing than the *carte du jour*. George apologized for being under strict dietary restraints. "But," he said, "I'm sure Beryl will find something in your wonderful meal that I can indulge in."

Lionel saw Beryl's look of panic as she surveyed the table. "Alicia," he said quietly, "do you realize that half of our guests are vegetarians and there is nothing green on this table?"

Alicia ignored the question since at that precise moment she remembered why she had put wine glasses on the table. She looked apologetically at her guests. "Would someone like to go below and fetch some wine? I ordered more of that Argentine stuff Groff's mother liked so much—"

Instantly Groff and Jack pushed back their chairs and volunteered to go to the wine cellar to get whatever there was that might take the edge off the menu.

They consumed a bottle of wine before they returned to the hardly-begun but nearly-completed meal.

The look Beryl gave her son was dirtier than the look Lionel gave Groff, the disproportionate show of admonition being occasioned by Groff's being, technically, the owner of the house. But both looks clearly conveyed disapproval. The two young men tentatively poked at the food until Groff, having come of age in more cosmopolitan areas of Europe, said flatly, "I can't eat this shit, Nana. I'm gonna order a pizza."

Lionel's phone vibrated. "You stay right where you are until I answer this!" He took the call and got up from the table, 'for privacy,' he said.

Everyone listened to Lionel's side of the conversation. He finally said, "He could use the experience and he has a friend with him who knows something about mechanics which might help. You never can tell. Three private investigators are at this very moment having dinner with me. I'll pass on the information and call you back within fifteen minutes, if any or all are willing to go. You, young man, need all the help you can get." He returned to the dining room.

Everyone pretended not to have been listening. Jack cut a huge wedge of cheese and tore a hunk of Stottle Cake. "This ain't bad," he said, encouraging Groff to try it.

"And this," Groff said, "ain't lamb! Nana, it's mutton. There's a big difference."

Alicia got up from the table and tearfully ran back to the kitchen. Lionel stared down his grandson. "When you do your clerking stint," he hissed, "I'm going to see to it that you do it in the Aleutian Islands!" He turned to go into the kitchen to comfort his wife, but Alicia had already come back to the dining room.

"You can at least try the Spotted Dick for dessert," she pleaded.

It was all too much for Lionel. He surrendered. "Spots on a dick cannot possibly constitute a dessert anywhere on the planet," he said, and everyone, even Alicia, began to laugh merrily.

It was an awkward prelude to the explanation of the legal aid he had just promised to give. He cleared his throat and continued. "The call I just had was from one Denis Lattimore, who is representing the granddaughter of a man who served under me in Viet Nam: Lieutenant Brendan Doyle, a man of courage and remarkable integrity, who died in combat. Many of us owe our lives to his uncommon valor. He received a Silver Star." Lionel sighed. "His granddaughter, a college girl named Tara Adams Doyle, has been charged with the murder of four people and the attempted murder of four others."

"Jesus!" George exclaimed. "How did she manage to do all that?"

"She's *alleged* to have poisoned them while she worked in the kitchen," Lionel defensively corrected him. "She's *alleged* to have fed them amanita *phalloides* mushrooms.

4

"The four people who succumbed to the poison were the cook, the cook's helper, and Tara's employers, Morley Madison Jr., and his wife, Jessica. Evidently, there is some old and bitter family history between the Madisons and the Doyles. Tara has been charged with murder in the first degree on the strength of a victim's death-bed statement that she vowed that night to annihilate the whole Madison line; but Lattimore feels sure he has successfully debunked that theory since it makes no sense. The Madisons have only two children and both were in another state at the time. As he put it, 'Killing a family without killing the children somehow fails the definition of eradicating an entire lineage for revenge, especially since the killer is likely to get only one bite of the *killing the whole family* apple.'"

Groff whistled. "Murder in the first degree. She's alleged to have poisoned them 'with malice aforethought'?"

"Yes. Premeditated. Lattimore is confident that not only will he get the 'murder one' charge thrown out, but he will also defeat the attempt to charge her with murder in the second degree. He further states that he's certain that this will be reduced to manslaughter in the first degree or possibly even the second degree; and he's confident that he can get her acquitted of even the lesser manslaughter charge."

"What were the circumstances?" Sensei asked.

Lionel consulted a notepad. "The Madisons gave a dinner party for a total of six people. They were celebrating the initiation of some business venture. Tara was asked to pick mushrooms for the sauce and they allege that she deliberately selected these poisonous amanitas. She's also charged with attempting to murder the four survivors who required immediate organ transplants which they obtained in India and in Taiwan. One liver and three kidneys. They are likely to be 'infirmed,' is the term he used, for the rest of their lives."

"What's the difference between murder degrees and manslaughter?" Jack asked.

Groff, aware that his grandfather was listening, tried not to sound like a law-student-expert. "Intent, principally. Manslaughter has two levels: voluntary, by a spontaneous response to being provoked, or the lesser involuntary, by a negligent act that caused the death.

"Murder in the first is planned... premeditated. Murder in the second is felonious murder. The homicide is related to the commission of another criminal act, or it was committed without premeditation but with a lethal weapon. Murder in the third degree is usually substituted with the manslaughter charges, homicide committed when the intent is to harm but not to kill. It's complicated because the rules and definitions vary from state to state. So do the sentences for each."

"Oh," said Jack. "So, with murder, the first is worst, and the third is least. That's the opposite of burns."

"Yes," Groff acknowledged, considering it. "Curious, isn't it."

Lionel restored the topic's trajectory. "My Lieutenant's granddaughter, Tara, was working in the kitchen. During the dinner's preparation, she's supposed to have argued with Mrs. Madison and the cook. This was immediately after she chopped onions and before she went out to pick the mushrooms. They had called her blind and stupid and made nasty remarks about her father, so the prosecutor contends that she reacted to their insults by deliberately picking some of the poisonous variety of mushrooms. Lattimore says that he will argue that anyone whose employer charges with 'being blind' has been given by that employer a reasonable defense against making an error in the selection of mushrooms. I didn't know whether to laugh or cry when I heard that one. But strange as it seems, it has a bizarre kind of merit. The prosecutor also says that she may have been grossly negligent in sorting out the mushrooms because she was hurrying to keep a date that she had early in the evening. She had agreed to pay the waiter, who served the dinner, to stay and help clean up the kitchen in her stead.

"Her grandfather was a fine man. Lieutenant Brendan Doyle. VMI. For those who may not know, that's Virginia Military Institute." Lionel looked at his grandson. "As a law student, you can't be expected to help with her defense beyond," he added harshly, "lending your epicurean insights into the preparation of the fatal meal." Satisfied that he had made his point, he continued, "Lattimore needs investigators. All that leg work costs money. So, George, Beryl, Sensei, and you, too, Jack, can you help out an old soldier? I'll donate to your employer whatever he owes you for your time and expense. I should add that the trial is next week. If you wish to help, you must help immediately."

Sensei shrugged. "Akara can cover the temple for me. He's staying in my guest room while I break him for priestly duty. So, sure, I can get away with no problem."

"Will he cover the office for us for a few bucks?" George asked.

"Give him the key to Beryl's apartment so that he can get to her Zen library, and he'll do it. But do they need all five of us to go?"

"I think they do," Lionel nodded. "There have been delays. A new judge now presides over the case and he wants it finished quickly. Everybody's in that 'clearing desks' mode before the July holidays and vacations."

"I'll go, if only to keep an eye on these two," Beryl said, indicating Jack and Groff. "And where, exactly, is this trial?" she asked.

"In rural South Carolina," Lionel answered, "near Columbia, a place on Lake Murray near Lexington, wherever that is."

"All five of us?" Groff asked warily. "This is gonna cost you big time, Grandpop."

"It's the least I can do," Lionel replied, wincing as he tried to chew the undercooked mutton.

MONDAY, JUNE 4, 2012

Groff drove the rented SUV from the airport in Columbia west on Route 378 as they skirted Lake Murray. It was late afternoon and the sun, setting directly in front of them, made them avert their eyes by looking sideways to glimpse the still, reflecting surface of the water. It was oddly quiet and, especially in the absence of a breeze, seemed at first to be as motionless as a painting. But a closer look revealed turtles wandering across the road or along it, birds flying down to rest on the places they had claimed in the trees, squirrels sprinting in all directions, a snake's head skimming across the water like an arrowhead, and an occasional fish "breaching" in fun or in the attempt to catch a low flying insect.

It had taken only an hour and a half to fly from Philadelphia to Columbia, but the flight had not lifted off until two o'clock; and by the time the five of them got organized and obtained the rental car, it was later than they had expected. They followed directions and hoped that they would encounter the town that reposed in a dell between lakeside and foothill. The town's name, Groff had already noted, was "Madisonville" and no doubt had a connection to the deceased dinner hosts, Morley Jr., Jessica, and to their son Morley, III and daughter Mariah, who both went to the same college as the defendant.

At six o'clock, a sexton rang the bell in a church that was somewhere nearby. They heard it clearly, but could not see even a spire until they followed a road sign's suggestion that they should turn right if they wanted to enter Madisonville. They turned, and another sign specifically said, "If you want to be welcomed in Madisonville, you best turn left up ahead." The road was gravel and traveling it was sufficiently slow for them to read the entire message as they passed. One final turn and there it was. "I hope," Beryl said, "there's a motel."

It was a small inn. The Madison Inn. At the desk Groff asked, "What accommodations do you have available?" And the clerk answered abruptly, "Only two, and a single lady must occupy one of them."

The remark was intended to discourage them from staying since four men could hardly fit in either of the available rooms; but Jack stepped forward immediately. "This lady is my mother," he said boldly. "And why, may I ask, must my mother be quartered in isolation? What are you suggesting?"

The clerk apologized. George's credit card was accepted, and after everyone's identity was verified and the register was signed, the clerk led them upstairs. Each room contained two single beds. Jack put his overnight bag on one of the beds in Beryl's room, and Sensei put his bedroll on the floor of the other room since he preferred, he said, to sleep on a hard, flat surface.

Dinner was remarkably good. Fresh broiled fish and steamed vegetables served with 'sweet' iced tea and fresh pineapple for dessert. George, still following the diet Beryl had sentenced him to, was permitted to eat everything that was served.

At seven o'clock, as they finished their meal, they were joined by attorney Denis Lattimore, a young man in his twenties who spoke with a peculiar southern accent. He pronounced his words by chopping them into syllabic segments that required the use of all recommended vowels. He seemed to say, "I'm" in two distinct parts: eye and yum. Everyone at the table stared at him with a piteous expression that conveyed more feeling for the fate of his client than his unfortunate manner of speech.

Lattimore took note of the stares. "My speech coach has done wonders helpin' me to lose my backwoods southern accent. Home-schoolin' doesn't purge the speech of colloquialisms and other unacceptable parochial dialects or, according to my dear mother, prepare a lawyer to argue before the Supreme Court of the United States, much less the Supreme Court of the State of South Carolina. Now, unless I'm excited, I say 'my' instead of 'mah.' I'm still not an accomplished rhotic speaker. Only strict self-discipline enables me to say 'speaker' instead of 'speakah.' It took a considerable amount of work but I have learned to pronounce that final "r" without soundin' like I'm growlin'. My voice coach asked me to give up tryin' to master that velar nasal terminal "g" since the harder I tried, the more I sounded Russian or Yiddish. Sleepink or drivink is simply not superior to sleepin' or drivin'."

George did not conceal his impatience. "You've a right to be proud of your many successes with the English language, but don't we have more important things to talk about?"

"Of course we do," Lattimore said, lowering his voice. "But every person who's not at this table is takin' note of everythin' that we're sayin'. You, Sir, are not in New York City where there are millions of individual minds and occupations. Here, in this village, there is, for all practical purposes, but one mind and one employer, and all eyes and ears serve the well bein' of that mind and employer. I speak of the Madison family. So, while you, here, are finishin' your supper, and they, there, are listenin' to our conversation, I will not use the occasion to lay out my case for them just to please your sense of urgency. Are we in accord?"

"I think so," George said, looking around and noticing for the first time that people were poised in the attitude of eavesdroppers.

"So," said Jack, "you've learned to pronounce the 'r' sound at the end of a word. And that's called 'rhotic.' That's commendable. Not in Boston, of course, but certainly around he-ah."

"May I suggest," Lattimore said, "that now that you all seem to have finished your meal, we go outside. It's light enough for me to show you around."

George nodded, stood up, and headed for the cashier's desk to sign the check.

Outside, they piled into the SUV and Lattimore pointed out the Baptist Church; the shops on Market Street; the stately courthouse; the sheriff's office and jail; and the volunteer fire department, all of which were notched out of the hillside as a ledge that seemed to make them vulnerable to a landslide. "I have learned," he announced, "that years ago the architect that Lieutenant Doyle commissioned designed a water run-off system consistin' of two channels that ran like a wish-bone that began above what was then called the 'Doyle House' down along the sides of the property - complete with picturesque bridges over them. Need I tell you that the Madisons dispensed with such common sense prophylaxis? I think not. Someday the top of this hill may rain down upon the middle, et cetera."

Between the commercial section and the lake were the residences of merchants, professionals, and administrators. "These folks," Lattimore confided, "whose lawns and public 'utility corners' are completely free of kudzu, are the ones who will likely duck jury duty because while they know that if they vote *in accordance* with the popular opinion their incomes won't be affected; but if they vote *against* the popular opinion, they will suffer for it financially - and may even be tarred and feathered and run out of town.

"The focal point of the hillside parabola is clearly the Madison Marina which had been built, fortunately," Lattimore intoned, "according to Doyle specifications. Doyle had envisioned a small harbor for unabashed owners of motorized vessels. The lake is usually too calm for sail, but you know these chauvinistic canvas people. Maybe it was just a 'thumb your nose at Annapolis' thing, but he wanted small vessels that used gasoline to feel welcome. Forty or fifty years ago this meant more than it does today."

The back of the elongated marina faced the town and politely acknowledged this by a flower-decked promenade for small shops that sold nautical garments, gift items, and the pottery and textiles of the State's few Native American tribes. Even the parking lot was beautiful, containing as it did many landscaped islands from which shade trees grew.

"You can't see the front of the marina," Lattimore said as though it were prohibited and not simply visible only from the water, "but it's all glass. The restaurant, bar, and sleepin' accommodations all have a wonderful view of Lake Murray." Three piers jutted into the lake. "The one on the left side is for docking... refueling and repairs. The houses on that side of the Marina are occupied mostly by the folks who work on the lake or on the boats or in any other manual or clerical labor. That's where your jury is gonna come from. The two other piers contain the slips for owners and visitors. And the houses on the right side of town are for folks who have lakeside homes in addition to their residences elsewhere. You can forget them... they don't vote hereabouts. The Madison Marina is owned by the Madison Development Company."

Lattimore directed Groff to drive uphill, past a small parking area, to the gated entrance driveway that led to three large houses that marked the extent of habitation on the hillside. "The center house is the one in which the incident occurred. Take a look and then we can drive back down to the little parking area. We can talk privately there."

Three plaques which individually gave the commercial names of the houses hung on the gate. "Notice how the house on the left is supposed to be modern in design. Marigolds line the driveway. They call it the 'Deer Run' model," Lattimore said, pointing to the sign. "I guess it is supposed to suggest *Bear Run* of Frank Lloyd Wright fame. The middle house is the Madison House. It looks antebellum with those big white columns and magnolia trees and Spanish moss hangin' on that one oak; but the war that house was built immediately before was Grenada. Pansies line the driveway. Why pansies? I do not know. But the house on the right is their 'York Minster' model. Can you believe it? They put a few tall thin stained glass windows in the facade and called it 'York Minster' which is the name of a cathedral. And they lined the driveway that goes to the 'York' model with miniature *red roses*. I am serious!"

"Does that recent construction date qualify them as *nouveau riche*, according to local criteria?" Groff asked.

"New?" Lattimore grunted. "What's before 'new'? The research and development phase? The house that Doyle designed was smaller and it allowed for the presence of many trees to hold the soil. The Madisons cut the trees down and built that comic book version of the Parthenon. Ronald Reagan was in the White House when they began the enlargement. Clinton was in when they dug the foundations for the other two houses. And they're all related, the occupants of the three houses. Notice, I didn't say 'owners.' The houses are owned by their real estate development company, a partnership called - now prepare yourselves - Madison Development Company." Lattimore giggled and then smiled triumphantly. "They are jointly and severally liable! They had several housing developments in the planning stage in other parts of the state, and they thought they'd be smart and call the houses 'models' to get some tax advantage. Their home owner's insurance carrier is not entirely sanguine about the perceived fraud."

"You mentioned 'liable,'" Groff said. "I guess they're going to be sued in civil court for damages that resulted from the poisoned dinner?"

"Oh, yes. And I only wish I had a piece of that action! The survivors and the families of the deceased have all retained counsel. They're pullin' every string they can find to hurry along this trial. And they're all prayin' I lose."

"Was it some kind of business dinner?" George asked.

"They were celebratin' the initiation of a natural gas extraction operation. In a beautiful area of South Carolina called Bosworth Hills, which is not far from here, a new middle-class housing development had been completely sold to hard workin' folks who were led to believe that their grant deeds gave them rights to the land down to the earth's liquid iron core. Too late did they discover that not only did they not own the mineral rights, but that the owner of those rights had viable 'rights of entry.' So the home owners merely owned their house and lawn... and I'm not entirely sure about the lawn.

"Now, the mineral rights to the land had been owned by a man who sold them last year to Morley Madison, Junior, and his wife Jessica who are two of the four individuals that Tara Doyle is accused of killin'. But by some strange reason, Morley Junior and Jessica sold those mineral rights to their two children, Morley III, and Mariah, last January, more than a month before the fatal dinner. Nobody seems to know why they did this. I'm lookin' into it. The transaction was quietly recorded. Neither Morley III nor Mariah was present at the poisoned meal.

"We're dealin' with three tiers of Madisons... the Morley Madison who was a contemporary of Tara Doyle's grandfather; the Morley

Madison Junior who was a contemporary of Tara's father; and Morley Madison III and his sister Mariah who are contemporaries and college mates of Tara.

"The middle Madisons - Morley Junior and his wife Jessica - contracted with a gas drillin' company named Stanfield; but they soon discovered it cost much more than they had estimated, so they had to seek investors. They found two couples who pledged large sums of money - hence, the occasion for the dinner, the proposed creation of *The Big Six*. There is, alas, no more talk of *The Big Six*. They are the six who sat down to what became the Last Supper, for two of them, anyway.

"It's been an eye-openin' experience. Many of us dug out the deeds to our domiciles and commenced prayin' that Hades had not seen fit to expel methane beneath our patios. I, fortunately, lease my condo, and the deed to my family's farm does convey the mineral rights." Denis Lattimore paused to look heavenward and reverently to close his eyes.

Beryl did not want to let the topic drop. "I'm curious about transferring the mineral rights to their children. I can see that parents might want to let their adult children get experience in business by giving them something to manage... you know, to learn the ropes of running a business. But then why weren't they at the dinner? There must be more to it."

Lattimore, recalled from his orations, looked at Beryl quizzically. "I don't think it was a secret thing... like one of those Chinese Tongs. I'm supposin' that the other members of the Madison Development Company - the in-laws who live in those nearby houses - didn't have the cash to invest. Possibly young Mariah and Morley III just didn't want to come. Kids find such dinners rather borin'. I do know that the other in-law members originally thought they'd be included, and I'm supposin' that the two investor couples wanted to limit the association to just their six. The in-laws are not what you'd call 'carriage trade.' They were somewhat miffed about being left out. They may have regarded this as a blessin' - at least until they learned that as owners of Madison Development they are liable for whatever resulted from that fatal meal. Torts, torts, and more torts. And I chose criminal law. Who knew?"

"Miffed about being rejected?" Beryl asked. "It's odd that they would go around telling people that. How did you find out?"

"My secretary, Miss Pattyanne Pastor, has reason to believe that the ladies who occupy the other two model homes purchased garments for the *soiree* - garments which they cannot now afford. Since the garments were altered, specifically to fit them, the shop owners are quite disturbed by this reversal of fortune. Apparently the ladies had also run up bills at the hair dressin' salon. Bleach, fingernails, and toenails... it all adds up. Rumor is that they complained to the shop owners about the perfidious nature of Morley and Jessica Madison when offerin' excuses for failin' to pay their bills. Miss Pastor is lookin' into it."

Lattimore had veered away from the topic. Beryl tried to get him back onto the original course. "How far did Morley and Jessica get with the original extraction effort?" she asked.

"Stanfield, the drillin' contractor for the natural gas extraction operation, moved all kinds of equipment onto the central park of Bosworth Hills. They started drillin' right there where the puttin' greens used to be. They put their office trailer on what was intended as an outdoor square dance floor. There was a pretty water fountain there that the driller's found right handy. Now Stanfield is in a grievous state of limbo. Torts!" Lattimore again looked heavenward.

"None of this," George noted, "really explains the case against Tara Doyle."

Groff Eckersley, imagining himself being grilled by his grandfather, protested. "I feel like a sock puppet," he said. "Somebody has to start moving his fingers. Four people killed and four people gravely injured! That should've been the stuff of network news. I never heard anything about it. So, what is this case really about?"

Lattimore was still answering to a higher authority. He continued, "I think it's important that you understand that Amanita *phalloides* poisonin' isn't one of these movie poisons in which the victim takes a bite, goes 'Aaaggah,' and falls dead. No, the Death Cap has an initial halcyon phase. Victims feel rather good after that delicious meal. They wipe their mouths and compliment the chef. And then, anywhere from

15

six to twelve hours after consuming the poison, the sickness begins. At first it looks like ordinary food poisonin'. The problem is that during the halcyon phase the victims may eat other meals and may tend later to hold those meals responsible for their distress. And then they waste time with over-the-counter medications: bicarbonate of soda, enemas, emetics. They are dying and just don't know it."

As they sat parked at the gate, night fell and it was necessary to put the SUV's lights on to go back down to the parking area. There, where Lattimore felt secure in speaking about his client, they opened the car doors. Immediately a breeze blew through, along with a few dozen mosquitos that seemed to favor George's after shave lotion.

Groff remained interested in Tara Doyle. "Can you give us an idea of Tara's personality? Her character? She plays varsity basketball. Does she have a jock mentality?"

"A jock mentality?" Lattimore was startled. "No, she plays basketball because she figured out long ago that she was too poor to afford the tuition. Tara Doyle abstains from all important social events; but invariably she is invited to them."

"Does she abstain because she can't afford the proper clothing?" Jack asked.

"Indeed. That is her reason. Nobody thinks of her as a jock. She, quite frankly, is disconcertin'ly intelligent. She's plain and sincerely humble. One of those *rara avis* types. I can tell you this: you won't like her and you won't not like her. You won't get close enough to make up your mind.

"As to the case, I'll be brief," Lattimore said. "With the exception of the cook and her assistant, the victims were on the verge of victimizin' a few hundred families. And that's what they were celebratin' at that feast of the ungodly.

"This dinner was on Monday, February 20th, which was a national holiday - President's Day. But the next day was Tuesday, or Mardi Gras, a day that is widely celebrated. Tara was hired to clean the house all day Sunday, the 19th. She was also hired as kitchen maid for the Monday evenin' dinner; and in case the weather turned bad and the guests did not leave on Monday evenin' as they planned, she had agreed to stay on as a chambermaid overnight.

"Tara attends college on a basketball scholarship and there was a big game on Monday, President's Day. She explained that nobody knows the exact moment a basketball game will end, but that she would leave the arena immediately and take the bus to Madisonville. She would be arrivin' around 3 p.m. Since the dinner wasn't going to be served until 7 p.m. that gave her plenty of time to help with the kitchen chores.

"The four guests were actually two couples who had been stayin' in Columbia. Each couple had its own limo, chauffeur, and valet. Before they started their drive to Madisonville late Monday afternoon, it had stopped rainin', but by dinner the skies were clear. Both couples planned to leave after dinner and drive at night to their destinations for the big celebrations on Tuesday.

"Now, all the servants of the four guests, that is to say, the two valets and two chauffeurs, had been together downstairs in the game room and were fed without incident. When the dinner ended, those servants naturally left with their employers. The Madisons' servants - that is, their cook, the scullery maid who also does light housekeepin', and the houseboy who went to college with Tara, all lived in the house.

"After Tara's basketball game, she rushed to get the bus and slipped and fell, strainin' her ankle. She didn't want to be late but she's also an athlete and couldn't take any chances, so she went to a nearby drugstore and got an Ace bandage and rented a couple of crutches. Then she called Mrs. Madison and told her that while she didn't think the injury was serious, it would cause an hour's delay. Since it was still rainin' she gave her employer the opportunity to tell her not to come, but Mrs. Madison said that bein' late was no problem. Tara got the next bus and arrived just before 4 p.m.

"The cook was makin' steak pies that contained vegetables and a mushroom and onion sauce fillin', but when Tara arrived, the mushrooms still hadn't been picked. The cook and the assistant were sittin' in the kitchen smokin' cigarettes, waitin' for Tara to go out to pick the mushrooms. The cook chastised her for being late and told her to first chop some onions so the cook could get the sauce started, and then to go out and gather as many mushrooms as she could find. They wanted lots of mushrooms. Tara chops the onions - they say they were scallions, which are much less pungent - and goes out into the woods behind the house and starts crawlin' around to collect the mushrooms.

"She brought them back and put them in a colander in the sink. The cook rinsed them while Tara went to clean up and change her clothes - she was dirty from crawlin' around outside - and she also had to put on a lady's maid uniform. She returned to the kitchen and was told to chop the mushrooms, which she did, and the cook added them to the onions in the saucepan."

Lattimore grew excited as he related the events. "The guests start to arrive, and Tara is sent out into the living room to help the ladies with their muddy shoes and to help the houseboy serve drinks and *hors d'oeuvres*. But every time she goes into the kitchen they insult her for one reason or another." He paused, to explain. "Mostly, they impugned her father's integrity. He had been an alcoholic but he'd been dead for years. Because of *his* father's heroic death, he was fatherless, and because of his mother's death, he was orphaned. He grew up poor, but not criminal.

"Tara was supposed to stay until the kitchen was clean, but her ankle had begun to hurt. She muttered an excuse about havin' another appointment and arranged to pay the houseboy twenty dollars to cover for her, and then she left."

"When did the poisoning become symptomatic?" Beryl asked.

"Ah," said Lattimore, "the pernicious mushrooms! The cook and the kitchen maid, who occupy separate rooms, begin to feel sick around 2 a.m. They get sicker and are startin' to have diarrhea and vomitin'. They each take their own 'tried and true' remedies for indigestion. When the distress worsens, they summon the houseboy Walter, who has already been awakened by the racket they're makin'. He's a vegetarian and didn't eat the pies. He sees that they're really ill, so he drives them right to Columbia General's emergency room. It's a holiday. They're busy in the E.R. He stays with the two women who are fast becomin' incoherent. An intern asks him if he knows what they ate recently, and he recites the menu. The women are immediately admitted, and Walter returns home. He admits to being astonished by the diagnosis of mushroom poisonin'. He says he knew that Tara, while no expert, had studied these fungi sufficiently to be able to distinguish edible from inedible. When he returns to Madison House, it's dawn and no one is home." Lattimore paused to take a deep breath.

Jack lowered his voice to a whisper. "Where was everybody?" he asked.

Lattimore sighed. "Well, let's see. After the guests left, the Madisons tried to de-compress over tea and some puddin' cake that had been left over from an earlier meal. They considered this dinner party a huge success and were plannin' their next triumph, and then they went to bed. Nobody disturbed them when the cook and the maid got sick. Walter figured they would prefer to be allowed to sleep and didn't disturb them.

"While he was gone, the Madisons began to feel sick. They stayed in their bedroom and tried the usual nostrums: bicarbonate of soda and bismuth and such - and after a few hours of increasin' discomfort, they went to awaken the servants but there's nobody there to take care of 'em. They don't know where anybody is so they have to wake up Jessica's brother - the one who lives in the 'Deer Run' model - and he calls for an ambulance that takes them to the hospital in Durbin, which is actually closer but in quite the opposite direction from Columbia.

"People can become rather irrational when they are in pain, and the absence of the staff didn't seem to bother the Madisons as much as their certainty that they had gotten food poisonin' from that puddin' cake.

"The guests had left at around nine o'clock in the evenin'. Two of them had gone to Raleigh, North Carolina. They drove the two hundred or so miles directly to a friend's home, arrivin' around one o'clock in the mornin'. Since their hosts were asleep, they told the servants not to disturb them. The cook kindly opened the kitchen and made them herb tea and club sandwiches. Then an hour or so later, maybe at three in the mornin', they began to feel sick. They didn't want to awaken the servants after having inconvenienced them already, so they tried to manage on their own with some antacid lozenges. By five o'clock they were in such distress that they awakened their hosts and complained bitterly how they had gotten sick after having eaten those club sandwiches. The cook was admonished. And once again it is proven that no good deed ever goes unpunished. The unfortunate pair was hospitalized in Raleigh. Both immediately flew to the Orient and each received a kidney. They did not require liver transplants as was first reported.

"The other couple had a similar experience. They drove the nearly three hundred miles to Jacksonville, Florida, but they stopped at a truck stop when a sudden squall came up. While they waited for the rain to abate, they had tea and eclairs. They arrived at their relative's house at three in the mornin'. They, too, complained about 'the bad eclairs' they had eaten at the truck stop. They thought they had salmonella poisonin'. They were all set to sue the truck stop and even went so far as to retain their own vomit in plastic bags as evidence. They were hospitalized in Jacksonville. They also went overseas immediately to get one liver and one kidney transplant.

"All four recovered without incident, but they won't be attendin' the trial... they've been stayin' near their respective hospitals in case there's any rejection problem.

"Regardin' delays and misinformation, what y'all need to remember," Lattimore said as an afterthought, "is that none of them had ever had the experience of Amanita *phalloides'* poisonin' before. It doesn't usually occur twice in someone's lifetime. Getting a reliable medical history is not always easy."

"Are mushroom poisonings common in these parts?" Sensei asked.

"There's different kinds of poison mushrooms," Lattimore answered. "We have cases, but they're rarely fatal. As to why this mass poisonin' didn't make network news, the answer is simple. The patients were in four different hospitals in three different states. The truth dribbled out for days. The dead didn't die all at once and the survivors were getting quick transplants in foreign countries. Of course, the authorities did put it all together, and Tara was charged."

"And they figured she deliberately picked the poisoned mushrooms?"

"That was their original theory of the crime. People died of eatin' poison mushrooms and Tara was the person who supplied them.

Naturally, the police investigation exposed that feud between the Doyles and the Madisons and the incontestable fact that Tara had studied toxic mushrooms in several of her college classes. It did not help that before the cook died she insisted that she overheard Tara swear that she was goin' to get even for the nasty remarks made to her in the kitchen. The scullery maid said she also heard Tara make that vow. The cook was quite dramatic. Oh, she suspected that those mushrooms were not quite right, but Tara had gone ahead and chopped them before she had a chance to examine them. And then, without askin', Tara added them to the sauce. This is a preposterous claim! Fortunately, the cook's revelations became even more irrational.

"The dinner guests didn't have much to say except that unlike most servants, Tara did not seem to enjoy her work. In video conference calls from their respective hospital beds, they described her manner as 'dour and indifferent.' With a charge like that," he grinned, "what could the District Attorney do?"

Groff took note: "The cook started the investigation by claiming that Tara deliberately poisoned them, but then she made her own testimony worthless by corrupting it with irrational claims; and, also I imagine, there's the obvious question of why, if she had heard Tara swear she'd get even and Tara had prevented her from examining the mushrooms, she didn't warn others or why she first attributed her own distress to simple indigestion."

"Exactly! They built their case on lies. They know it. Buck passin' and gossip. They've got to settle on manslaughter. And I'll fight that, too. Maybe the girl's vision was hampered by cryin' from all those hurtful insults, or the onions, or wet shrubbery slappin' her in the face. Or maybe somebody else did the poisonin'."

"What does Tara say happened?" George asked.

"She won't talk much about it. She says the mushrooms she picked were not poisonous. Period!"

"I'm interested in the victims," Beryl interjected. "How is it that the four guests did not die?"

Lattimore shrugged. "Luck, I guess."

21

"No... it couldn't have been luck," Beryl countered. "I don't know that it makes any difference to your defense of Tara, but it might make the jury more kindly disposed towards you if you determined the reason. People who take vitamins and supplements are always told that they are throwing their money away. Milk thistle, for example, is a common supplement that ordinary people use; but alcoholics and people who are getting radiation treatments are prescribed it in fairly large amounts because it assists the liver in detoxifying poisonous substances."

"Ah." Lattimore opened his laptop computer and net-searched "milk thistle." To his astonishment the first article he read recommended its use specifically for Amanita *phalloides* poisoning. "It certainly won't hurt my image to give to the folks information they can use."

"What is it that we're supposed to do?" Jack inquired.

"I need character witnesses, details about the Doyle-Madison feud, verification that Tara played on President's Day and was subsequently seen on crutches, and above all, who else could possibly have poisoned that meal... who, how, why and when. The Madisons were not friendly folks. They surely had enemies. I need alternate suspects. Who else wanted them dead? Who else besides rejected relatives and the hundreds of residents of Bosworth Hills who were gonna' be financially destroyed by the folks at that dinner? Who else besides those other hundreds of homeowners that The Big Six were targetin' around the state?

"And you, Miss Beryl, I need that girl to come to court lookin' like Little Miss Muffet, not like a pro wrestler havin' a bad hair day. She dresses like a boy, a sloppy boy. Clean her up. And she ain't out on bail. That will mean buyin' her clothing. So you'll have to do her hair and makeup, yourself."

George did not want to discuss fashion or good character. "I'd like to know why none of this has been done yet. Why has it taken so long to get us involved in this trial?"

"I got this case five weeks ago," Lattimore answered. "When Tara was first arrested in March, another attorney had been appointed. He got one of those 'pro bono' heart attacks. Spent a couple of hours in the E.R. to prove it. So there I was, mid-April, blowin' the ink dry on my license to practice law. I was new to town. I'm from rural Spartanburg.

I'd rented office space, but had, as yet, no desk or chair. I had to get my office set up. I had to hire a secretary. I became Tara's attorney when I walked into a courtroom and the judge pointed a finger at me. That was it. One does not argue with a judge."

George nodded sympathetically. "One doesn't usually win if one does."

"When I familiarized myself with the case, I automatically scoffed at the first degree murder charge. And then I got my first lesson in courtroom politics. The prosecutor indicated that he had gotten a better look at things and just might reduce the charge to manslaughter, so when he asked that, for the sake of the witnesses, the trial be held in the vicinity of the crime, I didn't want to spoil things by being contrary. The judge agreed and the venue was set. Hah! Nobody said that the immediate vicinity was named Madisonville. Who knew? Once I saw the prejudicial climate in this little town, I tried to get a change of venue. I failed. Unfortunately we were alone together when the judge's clerk said to me, 'No matter where you go in South Carolina people who poison other people get a fair trial.'"

"I feel your pain," Groff said.

"Meanwhile, I needed a secretary and as luck would have it, the Good Lord sent Miss Pattyanne Pastor to me. I still cannot believe my good fortune. Imagine, a secretary who is *experienced in law*.

"Everything was rushed. Miss Pattyanne Pastor told me to insist upon a delay; but I was a fool. What was I doing? Making mantras out of 'Justice delayed is justice denied' or 'To get along, go along'? I was in over my head.

"Then I received an anonymous call tellin' me to contact your grandfather. The gentleman had also served with Brendan Doyle years ago. He said to me, 'Doyle is dead and buried in the earth. But he's very much alive to some of us. In his name, help the girl.' Two days later I received an envelope in the mail with two thousand dollars in it. No note. No return address. I hadn't intended to call a lawyer in Pennsylvania to ask for help, even though I truly needed it. But that money changed my mind. A stranger was her champion. And, shame on me! I was supposed to be her champion. I called Mr. Eckersley."

TUESDAY, JUNE 5, 2012

Every table was taken when Beryl and Jack came down for breakfast. They stood in an alcove that was reserved for waiting customers; and within ten minutes, Sensei, George, and Groff came down at the same time that Denis Lattimore pulled into the parking lot.

When they were seated in the crowded room, they felt safe enough only to discuss the weather, European politics, and the paintings of Gerhard Richter. Finally, without lingering over coffee, they went immediately to the little parking area above town to hear Denis Lattimore review their assignments.

"Miss Tilson," he began, "I'd like you to come to the jail to meet our client, get measurements, and see what you need to create a wardrobe, makeup, and hair style.

"Jack and Groff, I'd like you to go into Columbia and find Tara's friends, her coach and teammates, and her professors. When you interview one, be sure to ask up front if he or she would be willin' to testify to Tara's good character. Be sure to ask first. People love to talk but hate to testify. See what you can learn that we can use. Get the negative stuff, too. We don't want surprises.

"George, how about interviewin' Walter, the houseboy, and the other members of the Madison family who were not invited to the dinner and who are now going to lose everythin' in that maelstrom of civil actions. You're the professional. You know what buttons to push to get information.

"I've lined up a friendly psychiatrist who will testify to her gentle and cooperative disposition, providin' she'll get off her high horse long enough to speak to him. I'll see about gettin' the lab tests done on the other ingredients that were used in the meal's preparation in case one of them was poisoned. As my 'fall-back' position, since Tara wears glasses, I've contacted an eye specialist to testify that between grief, onions, and wet shrubbery slappin' the lenses, she could easily have erred.

"Sensei, you're supposed to be a martial artist. I'm guessin' that you know somethin' about body language."

"Yes," Sensei said. "I know something about it."

"Then come with Beryl and me to the jail and we'll try to get Tara to talk about that awful night. She may say more with her limbs than she says with her tongue."

Tara Doyle sat in her cell, reading a paperback copy of *Finnegan's Wake*.

To accommodate the sanctity and privacy of attorney-client communication, Deputy Sheriff Pelley wheeled an old typing table and two chairs into the corridor in front of the cell and closed the hallway door that led to the outer office. Beryl asked if she could pass a yellow plastic measuring tape through the bars to the prisoner. The deputy looked at the tape and, pronouncing it "possibly dangerous," said that he would give the prisoner a piece of string and she could measure whatever she liked. Beryl could then place the string against the tape in the corridor's safe environment. He went to his desk to get a spool of thread.

Tara asked, "What is it you wish to measure?"

The question surprised Beryl. "Bust size. Waist. Waist to shoe vamp. Length and width of foot. Hips. The usual. I'm going into Columbia to get you clothing to wear to court."

"What I have is fine," said Tara, taking a martyr's attitude. "You need not buy me anything."

Beryl, already piqued by the 'dangerous' measuring tape, was not inclined to coddle the prisoner. "Look," she said, "if you want to be an anti-prima donna, that's fine with me. Maybe you think poor clothing will make the jury sympathize with you. It won't. They'll think you're a slob who didn't give a rat's ass about what kind of mushrooms you put in the sauce. And that's fine with me, too. But making this good man–" she indicated Denis Lattimore, "lose a case that he might otherwise have won but for your appearance, is not fine with me. So take the bloody string and measure yourself."

Deputy Pelley raised his eyebrows. He extended the spool of thread through the bars. "I'd cooperate if I was you," he said.

Tara wrapped the thread around her waist and pinched the point where it met the thread's end. The deputy handed her a felt pen. "Mark it," he said.

It required a half hour for Beryl to get all of the measurements. She was not in a good mood when she left the jail alone and returned to the Inn.

"Tara," Lattimore began, "this is Sensei Percy Wong from Philadelphia. He's here to help us with your defense. We're tryin' to get the charge reduced to involuntary manslaughter. You'll have to help us."

Tara said nothing.

Lattimore continued. "The difference to you is freedom or years in prison."

"I'm sorry about that," Tara said, resuming her position beside the window. "In or out of jail, I'm determined to get my degree." She picked up her book.

Tara Doyle had begun the second half of her junior year in January and by March, when she was arrested, she had helped the women's basketball team to achieve a place in the playoffs for state championship. Her absence was keenly felt and they lost in what was called, "a rout." Her classmates rallied to her cause and with the assistance of her professors, all the class lectures were video-recorded and replayed by an accommodating warden in the jail's recreation room. She was also permitted to keep text books in her cell providing the covers were removed - a precaution against secreting anything between the spine and the hard cover's spine-extreme, a place known to be used for concealing a contraband knife or drug.

At semester's end, she had passed all her classes.

While nearly everyone in Madisonville believed her to be guilty, nearly no one in Columbia who knew about the case thought that she could possibly have done such a thing. Their assurance affected her judgment. She began to view her problems with the certitude of acquittal. She exercised in her cell and played in the outdoor basketball court, preparing to rejoin her team in the fall. But then she was moved to Madisonville, and for several weeks she languished in the little cell feeling a palpable hostility that rubbed off all her previous confidence. She adjusted her expectations and seemed resigned to her fate.

Lattimore tried again. "Miss Doyle! Please! We must have your cooperation."

She slowly removed her gaze from the book and looked at Lattimore. "Perhaps later. I'm very busy right now."

Sensei pulled Lattimore aside. "Let George talk to her," he whispered. "I'll interview Walter and anyone else on his list. We'll be meeting soon at the Inn. We can rearrange our assignments there."

Lattimore snapped his briefcase shut. "I, for one, will be damned glad to see this business concluded. I, too, have a life."

As they turned to leave, Sensei asked, "I neglected to ask. Are you married?"

"No," said Lattimore. "But my parents are assurin' everyone that their precocious son is goin' to get that girl acquitted. Especially my father! Do you have a father who would like to use you as his sword and shield?"

"Not any more," Sensei said. "Not any more."

Since Jack and Groff had taken the SUV into Columbia, Beryl thought that she would try to get Tara a few appropriate garments locally, in the event that she would be called into court unexpectedly. She strolled down Market Street, looking for a shop that sold ladies' clothing. There was only one such shop and the window display made it clear that the style preferred by the owner was "Sunday Go To Meeting." Beryl went in and searched the racks for something that could be restyled into a garment suitable for a courtroom. Finally she found a powder blue linen suit that was inexplicably trimmed with white lace. An inch of gathered lace protruded from the collar, cuffs, lapels, and hem. With care and her good cuticle scissors she could easily remove the trimmings. She bought a white purse and shoes with medium size heels. "Even if they pinch," she told herself, "she'll only have to walk from one building to the next." She also bought underwear and stockings and a white plastic bracelet and matching necklace. She returned to the Inn to find Sensei and Denis Lattimore having coffee in the dining room.

"The boys," she announced, "won't be back from Columbia until this evening. I got Tara one outfit but I'll have to drive into town with them tomorrow to get more. I'll rent another car while I'm there."

"We're goin' to ask George to go with me this afternoon," Lattimore announced. "Sensei, here, thinks George can get her to cooperate better than I. I can't get her to cooperate at all."

"She is one funny duck," Beryl agreed, looking out the window to see George walk slowly towards the Inn's entrance. "I should have told you that George was shot in the knee when he was a police detective. He can't easily walk any distance. The walk up the hill seems to have taken him to his limit. Fortunately, the courthouse is close by."

George Wagner came in and sat at their table. "Nobody would talk to me at the Madison House. Walter is staying here in town at the Marina.

"At the Deer Run Modern House, the kids are all away for the summer and the parents didn't want to speak without their attorney being present. They said as soon as they could make some kind of arrangement, they'd let me know."

"That's more than I got out of them," Lattimore sighed. "They wouldn't even answer the door for me. I'm supposed to have rights."

"What about the York Minster House?" Beryl asked.

"Jessica's sister and her husband didn't want to talk, either. They did say that if their attorney was agreeable they would consider a video conference call of some kind."

"Let's eat lunch," Beryl said, "and afterwards George and Denis can go to the jail, Sensei can run down Walter - assuming he's in town - and I will carefully remove the idiotic lace from the suit I bought Tara. Then I'll go to the drugstore and get curlers, hair spray, and makeup."

Groff Eckersley and Jack Tilson did not imagine that their good looks had anything to do with being granted an interview with a female in authority. They approached a secretary and, affecting the casual swagger of movie detectives, tried to seduce her with hard-boiled *savoir faire*. The secretary giggled and called her boss.

Chelsea College's head of women's athletics, Jamie Haloran, Ph.D., was masculine in her manner and dress. She wore a diagonally striped tie that Jack immediately admired. "Rep ties are coming back, big time," he said. "GQ is full of 'em."

"You know," mused Groff aloud, "I have a tailor in Milan who insists that the little stitches on the back of the tie, if it's a good tie - next time you take it off check to see those little stitches - should be snipped before you have it cleaned, so that they have to clean and press the tie completely flat. Then you can either tack the sides together yourself or take it back to your tailor and he'll tack it and gently press the sides down. I thought he was nuts, but it does make a difference." He and Jack sat down in the two chairs that were positioned in front of her desk.

"Well," said the head of women's athletics, "this is a good tie. It was a gift. Women have a worse problem keeping ties clean than men have, especially when they're stout like me. It's this damned bustline. The tie lays out there at a forty-five degree angle. You can't drop anything on your lap. Oh, no. Right away it's on your tie."

"Bummer," said Jack.

"What can I do for you gentlemen?" she asked. "And what are your names, by the way?"

Groff stood up to get his wallet out of his jeans' pocket. "I apologize, Doctor Haloran," he said. "I'm not used to assignments of this pleasant sort." He removed his engraved personal card from a card-case inside his wallet and handed it to her. He looked down at Jack. "Where's your card?"

"I don't have a card," Jack protested. "What kind of idiot runs around with a card? Jesus! Is Oscar Wilde or Beau Brummel gonna walk in here next?"

Doctor Haloran read, "Groff Zollern Eckersley, The Hollyoak, Chester County, Pennsylvania." She looked up at him. "What do you do, Groff Zollern Eckersley, besides spend your time being Groff Zollern Eckersley?"

"Just being *that* is both my vocation and my avocation," he answered, smiling. "Actually, I'm a law student and my grandfather volunteered me for all those ancillary services defense attorneys require in preparation of a case. I'm technically an agent of Denis Lattimore in the matter of the State of South Carolina versus Tara Doyle. And this person sitting here without the proper means of introduction, that is to say, a calling card, is Jack Tilson. He's getting his master's in mechanical engineering at Arizona State. He has no cause to waste time being Jack Tilson in any capacity, which does render him free to fix your car or refrigerator or anything mechanical you have that's broken."

Jack grunted. "You are breaking Dr. Haloran's heart. She once had hope for the human race. As of two minutes ago, she no longer has."

"Pay no attention to him, Ms. Jamie," Groff said.

Jack sat up. "If you ask if you can call her 'Jim,' I'm leaving!"

Dr. Haloran grinned and shook her head. "Whatever you want, you can have." She picked up a tissue and began to wave it. "I surrender."

Groff asked, "Would you be willing to sign the Instrument of Surrender in Madisonville after you testify to the all-around excellence of Tara Doyle? And if we ask her associates to testify and they agree - pending your approval, of course - would you further encourage them to testify likewise at the same proceeding?"

"I will so testify and I can assure you that many people will happily testify to Tara's gentle demeanor, her generosity and her abilities as a team player," she laughed as she continued to recite the litany of cliches, "her modesty and her dignity, her dedication to the refinements of scholarship, and to her being the most unpretentious and most cooperative young lady of all those who attend Chelsea - or who ever have. Will that do?"

"Perfectamundo," said Jack. "You're making our search for character witnesses an exciting adventure."

"You are a peach," Groff said quietly.

"There's just one thing," Dr. Haloran said. "How do you keep linen pants from creasing?"

She was teasing Groff, but he took her question seriously. "Wear a very tight girdle," he said. "That will keep your skin's natural moisture and pressure away from the fabric. If you perspire though the undergarment, spray the inside of the pants with waterproofing spray - the sort they use on raincoats. You won't stop all of the creasing but you will stop most of it... at least, that's been my experience."

Jack leaned back in his chair and scoffed, "Like... you wear a girdle when you wear linen pants?"

"I used to, of course, but that was before I got my Prince Albert." He winked at Dr. Haloran who put her head down on the desk and waved the tissue.

When she looked up again, she said, "I will certainly follow your advice." After a few "after shock" giggles, she reminded them of a detail they had overlooked. "And I suppose that I should notify Lattimore's office here in town that I will happily be a witness, and I should ask all the others each to notify his office of the same?"

"Yes," Groff said. "You'd all have to be put on a witness list. And as soon as possible, if you would..."

"Could you recommend a good restaurant?" Jack asked.

"Here!" She opened her desk drawer and removed two forms. "You can have lunch on me in the faculty dining room. Don't worry. The food is good."

After lunch they went to the gym and shot hoops with a few straggling male players. A whistle blew and the men left the court. What was left of the women's basketball program entered. Jack and Groff remained.

The women's coach asked them who they were and what they were doing there. Groff shouted his answer. "We're on Tara Doyle's defense team. We're working for Denis Lattimore, her attorney. Do any of you ladies know Tara personally?"

They all did.

"Then allow me to rephrase that," said Jack. "Which of you knew her best, off the court?"

Two girls stepped forward and led Jack and Groff to the benches while the rest of the women resumed their basketball drills.

"I'm Nancy deWitt," said the blonde, "and my red headed friend here is Patricia Galsworthy."

Groff, minus the card, introduced himself and Jack.

"So," said Groff, "we're told that Tara hated the Madisons and vice versa. What was the story from Tara's point of view? Can you give us the history of the feud?"

"How much time do you have?" Nancy asked.

"Hey! I'm sittin' here between two beautiful Southern Belles," Jack said. "Does anyone think I give a damn about the time it takes?"

"Fortunately," she replied, "we don't have to go back to the War of Northern Aggression. In these parts, historical accounts usually include that event. Well," she sighed, "since my family has lived in Columbia for generations, I'll try to answer as informatively and as succinctly as possible. The Doyles are an old and proud family. We can show you the splendid house they once called home, if you want to meet us after practice."

"Of course we want to meet you after practice... and see the Doyle house, too," Groff said.

"You probably don't need to go back any farther than Brendan Doyle, Tara's grandfather," Nancy began the narrative. "Now, the Doyles once had a cotton plantation, but when they ran out of 'stay-at-home' male heirs, they sold it. They then had a construction business and the first Morley Madison was an employee of theirs. Brendan was an only child and when he went away to VMI, the Doyles treated Morley like a son. When Brendan graduated, he had a big summer wedding. Everybody who was anybody attended. He wanted to build a home for himself and his new wife on Lake Murray and operate a small marina there, so he bought a large tract of land. His new wife had some nautical business experience and he hoped it would give her a little financial security. The land went from the lake over the hill and down again to the road. It was a dirt road in those days. Route 378. Maybe it was asphalt, I'm not sure.

"Brendan gets the work started. He has the architect and all that paperwork and the mortgage lined up, and then he's notified that he's going to Viet Nam. So Morley continues the project. Brendan wants it done because his wife is pregnant and she doesn't get along with his parents. She was from Connecticut.

"And then while Brendan's away, Morley is in danger of being drafted. And suddenly Brendan's parents grew sick, and when Morley was called up, he claimed to be vital to the national defense. He said that his job - they were building some kind of government installation - a post office, I think - was indispensable and that he also had to care for Mr. and Mrs. Doyle. Lots of others were joining the ROTC, which my daddy says used to mean, Run Off To Canada but it really means something else. But it was for college boys and Morley never got beyond high school.

"And then everybody started dying at once. Brendan was killed in combat, and I guess that didn't help whatever was ailing the Doyles, because as soon as Morley got his deferment, they died. First Mrs. Doyle and then her husband. She was from Charleston and wanted to be buried there. Morley arranged it. And then when Mr. Doyle died, supposedly of natural causes, Morley had his body shipped there too. My father says they ought to exhume the bodies. He says Morley probably poisoned them."

"Does he have any proof?" Groff asked hopefully.

"Honey, people need instincts, not proof. At least that's the way things are around here," Patricia said.

Nancy resumed her story. "When Brendan's body is returned, which I think was right after his parents died, Morley wants to ship him off to Charleston, too. But the local gentry quietly arrange for him to have a hero's funeral and be buried in our cemetery. Brendan's wife is half out of her mind with grief. She has a baby boy. Right away, Morley starts needing to see her about the Lake Murray project. Next thing anybody knows, there's a balloon payment due and contractors' liens are placed against the property. Brendan's widow is really crazy now. And Morley Madison comforts her the old fashioned way, and she's soon somewhat pregnant and thinks they're gonna' get married, and I guess she signed anything he put in front of her. Imagine her surprise when he produces a wife and kids that he's had all along in some town outside Boston. My daddy says that they spoke English like it was a foreign language. Nobody could understand a word they said. And as fast as you can say 'Robert E. Lee,' Morley owns the entire property and the construction company, too.

"Brendan's widow has nobody to turn to. Nobody knows where her parents were, up there in Connecticut. A wedding's supposed to take place in the bride's home not the groom's. So maybe she didn't have any parents. But the next thing that happens is that she dies of infection after she tries to have an abortion which was sort of illegal in those days. My father says he took advantage of her because he wanted the thrill of layin' with a hero's wife. My father says she was like Igraine in *La Morte d'Arthur*. Bewitched. Morley hated that Brendan was superior to him in every way. My father says Morley Madison was a carpet baggin' thug from Massachusetts.

"But anyway, Morley brought his kids and his truck-stop wife to town. She had delusions of grandeur and wanted to live in the old Doyle house. But the neighbors saw to it that it was tied up in court for the longest time, so they had to live in another part of town. An old spinster in the Doyle family took charge of that baby boy who became Tara's father. She lived in a cottage that's gone now.

"The Madisons redesigned the house on the lake that Brendan had planned and they eventually moved in. By then Morley owned everything the Doyles had ever owned. And his son became the Morley Madison, Junior, who just had a nice Death Cap for dinner. He married Jessica who is also white trash and they have two kids, Morley III and Mariah, who think they are so superior to everyone. They go to college here in this very institution. My daddy says that they'd go to school in Massachusetts if it weren't for the pleasure they got from drivin' to class here in their foreign sports cars. Massachusetts is in our debt."

"Wait a minute," Jack showed his palm, signaling that she should slow down. "Where does Tara's father fit into all of this?"

"He lived with that spinster aunt on money he got for being a veteran's son, but he was emotionally lost. She was an odd old lady and didn't know how to raise a boy. He couldn't stay in school since he'd have these fits of depression. People got tired of trying to help him, and when he was old enough, he became a notorious drunk. Actually, he was an alcoholic before he was old enough to drink legally. Seriously!

"But he did marry a lady from a very good family, Miss Annabel Adams, who was twice his age, and her family disowned her for that. I mean, society has rules! Tara is the only child he ever had, that we know of, anyway. He died when Tara was ten or eleven, a year or so before the turn of the century, 2000 that is. She adored him. And he loved her too. He used to read poetry to her. He didn't have any life insurance or anything. It was really hard for them. Her mother was old, and bein' a lady, she had no skills. She lived with Tara in a boardin' house in a nasty part of town. Tara worked in the kitchen to pay for their room and board, and because she was tall, she began to play basketball with the neighborhood boys. She knew that was her ticket to our rather expensive college, which is where she belonged! So she got good at basketball. And then her mom died of," she lowered her voice, "cancer."

Groff sighed. "Does everybody know this history? Is it common knowledge or is it just knowledge that people who are in society know?"

"This is *not* common knowledge! No. You'd have to have ancestors in town who were alive and social at the time."

Jack wanted to be sure of the information's exclusivity. "Do any of the girls on the basketball court now know this story?"

"No. Certainly not. I mean, I'm not going to tell them. They're all from good families, but not local ones. Tara should have been a debutante. She may be poor but society isn't just about money, is it?"

Jack grinned suspiciously. "Then how is it you told us so easily?"

"Why, Doctor Jaime Haloran is a descendant of Jefferson Davis! She checked you out! She said that you were genteel and honorable northerners and it was perfectly all right to talk to you."

Groff laughed. "So you knew who we were when you came in here?"

"Of course," Patricia said. "Honey, good breedin' is a grape vine, and news does travel along it rather quickly."

"And we're just grapes on the vine," Groff grinned.

"Yes, and now you are officially on the vine." She put her hand on his cheek and then quickly looked around to be sure that the gesture had not been witnessed by the coach.

"Do either of you think she's guilty of the crime?" Jack asked.

"If the Madisons were the only dead diners, she'd be feted not charged."

"Did she ever complain about the way the original Morley Madison had swindled her grandmother out of that land?"

"Not aloud. But every day off that she got, if there was a little wind, she'd rent a small sailboat and sail all the way to the marina there on the lakeside property that her grandfather once owned, the property the Madisons cheated her grandmother out of. She'd drop anchor and stare at the beautiful landscape there. She loved that big piece of land. Then she'd sail back. Now she's there again, in jail."

"Well," said Groff, "any chance of you gals skipping the rest of practice right now and showing us the house?"

"Why sure, Hon, on one condition."

"Anythin', Darlin'," Groff grinned.

"That you'll let us drop this stereotypical 'southern airhead' manner of speakin'."

Patricia added, "Do your Philadelphia womenfolk simper in such an equally objectionable manner?"

"No," Jack said. "They do not. And far from finding it objectionable, I find it hot. *Tres* hot. *Muy* hot. You should start a school up there, a 'Simpering Academy.'"

"Hell," Groff yelled. "I'd sign up."

The girls laughed and went to obtain permission to leave. Groff turned to Jack. "They're gonna need coaching if they take the witness stand. We'll have to talk to Denis."

"I got it," said Jack. "With no effort at all they'd supply the prosecution with lots of 'motive.'"

In the jail's "cellblock" hallway, George Wagner sat on a bench beside Denis Lattimore. Tara Doyle stubbornly lay upon her bed.

George used his avuncular voice. "Come on, girl," he said. "I'm here at the request of one of your grandfather's 'comrades in arms.' Lionel Eckersley knew your grandfather in Viet Nam. Brendan Doyle made such an impression on him that decades later as soon as he heard you were in trouble, he sent five people down here to help with your defense. The least you can do is talk to us."

Tara closed her book. "I've read the same page two hundred times and still don't understand what I'm reading. I think I'll save it for a more auspicious occasion." She dragged a stool to the bars and sat down. "What do you want to know?"

George began his "interrogation." He gently asked, "How did you come to be employed at the Madison House?"

"Walter told me they were having a dinner party and needed extra help. Walt goes to college in town, but he lives at the Madison House. He takes the bus into town on Monday morning and goes back again on Wednesday afternoon. That's his 'weekend off' time. He has friends who tape the lectures he misses. He takes business and psychology courses. No labs or anything. Madison House is busiest on weekends. Anyway, he told me about the dinner party."

"When was this?"

"The dinner was on Monday, February 20th, President's Day. He asked me on the Wednesday before then. So let's see, Monday the 20th, Sunday the 19th, Saturday the 18th, Friday the 17th, Thursday the 16th, Wednesday the 15th."

"After he asked you, did he return to Madison House as usual?"

"I didn't see him get on the bus, but I suppose he did." She grinned. "I assume he didn't flap his wings and fly there."

"What hours were you supposed to work?"

"Hmmm. I was supposed to work all day Sunday, cleaning the house. They were getting the place ready for the big party and it was a kind of 'spring cleaning' effort. Washing windows, taking all the books off the shelves to dust them properly."

"But you were there on President's Day. What hours were you supposed to work on President's Day?"

"I played basketball on President's Day. So I don't know what hours I was *supposed* to work. I just let Mrs. Madison know that I had no way of telling what time the game would end. I mean, you can't be specific about the time that the final buzzer goes off. There are all kinds of delays: foul shots, time outs."

"So what time did you tell her that you would be there? Approximately."

"I was told that if I got there in the vicinity of three o'clock it would be acceptable. I was hurrying to the bus stop. It was raining and I fell and twisted my ankle. I'm an athlete and a twisted ankle is nothing to ignore. But I needed the pay. I was going to be paid for both days on Monday. I called to let her know I was running late."

"And she agreed to let you come late?"

"Yes. Obviously. She didn't throw me out when I got there. Yes, it was maybe three forty-five when I got there. Rain slows everything down. Even the bus doesn't go as fast. Naturally, it was raining in Columbia the same as it was raining in Madisonville."

"You had to leave her house early. Did she know about that?"

"Did she know I had to leave early? What was early as far as the dinner was concerned? They were all eating the main course when I left. And the dessert was ice cream already dished out and waiting in the big freezer. All the staff had to do was carry it in. So aside from clearing the table of the main course's dishes, everything was done. And clearing the table was not my responsibility."

"Was Mrs. Madison ok with your leaving early?"

"I left so I can't say what she was. I guess so. My ankle hurt me so bad I just had to leave."

"Tell us about the mushrooms. Were you asked to pick a certain variety?"

"I wasn't asked to do anything. I was ordered to go out in the rain and pick as many as I could."

"Were you hampered in any way?"

"Sure I was hampered! After I hurt my ankle, I went to a drug store and got an Ace bandage for it, and I rented crutches to keep from putting weight on my foot in case something was seriously wrong. I didn't want to make it worse."

"Did you use the crutches in the kitchen?"

"I couldn't very well work on crutches in the kitchen, could I?"

"So you had no crutches when you went out to gather the mushrooms."

"What good would crutches do out there in the mud and loam where the mushrooms grow? A person doesn't crawl on crutches."

"Do you know a Death Cap when you see one?"

"I know enough not to test my knowledge by eating one that I have doubts about."

"But you picked enough of them to kill eight people."

"It doesn't take many Death Caps to kill an Army."

"Did you recognize them in the woods?"

"It was dark in the woods."

"But it wasn't dark in the kitchen when you chopped them."

"I was using the same cutting board and chopper that I used on the onions. Maybe they made my eyes tear-up."

"They said 'scallions' not onions."

"They can say whatever they like. Scallions are tubes and have long green, tail-like leaves. These were not scallions."

"What did they say when they saw you crying in the kitchen?"

"They laughed. They thought they had succeeded in hurting my feelings. But it was my ankle that was hurting and my eyes that were watering from the onions. And while I was crawling around out there in the bushes I kept getting slapped in the face. So they can take all the credit they want for making me cry. But my ankle, the onions, and the shrubbery are what made me cry."

"What did the cook or Mrs. Madison say about your father?"

"What did Mrs. Madison say? Only that if there were any sauce left over I should ask the cook for it... so that I could put it on the roadkill my father would be serving for dinner. But I didn't pay much attention to it. It was one of those remarks that were intended to discipline me... the way a drill sergeant insults new recruits."

"And the cook and the assistant? They said something nasty, too, as you were leaving."

"I'm sure they did. I don't remember what, specifically. Too bad we can't ask them."

"Would they deny it?"

"Oh, yes. Probably. They hear what they want to hear. And if it helps them, they hear you say things you never said. That's the way they do things. Lie and swear to it."

"Did anyone else hear it?"

"How should I know?"

"Where was Walter?"

"Why are you asking me to account for his whereabouts? He's not just a waiter, he's the houseboy, the butler, everything. He could have been anywhere. Maybe he heard it. Ask him."

"So, as far as you knew, the steak pies were safe to eat."

"I'd have eaten one if they had made one for me. My ankle hurt so bad that I had to leave to attend to it. I'm an athlete. My legs are important to me. If I didn't leave when I did, I'd be dead, too. Is that all you want to know? I think I've answered enough questions." She covered her mouth. "I'm not saying another word."

"Ok, Tara. Thank you for your time." George got up.

Lattimore told her to keep her chin up, then he and George left.

Sensei found Walter in the parking lot of the Marina Club.

"I'd like to ask you a few questions," he said. "I'm working for Denis Lattimore on the Doyle case."

"Not without my lawyer being present." Walter waved him off with a dismissive flick of his hand. He turned his back to Sensei and opened his car door.

"When can I make an appointment?" Sensei was suddenly angry.

"Are you at the Inn?"

"Yes. Ask for Percy Wong. I need to talk to you."

Walter did not step into the car. Instead he stood there with the door open and yelled, "Don't threaten me! I'll have you arrested!" As people turned to look, his expression changed into a smirk, and he entered his car.

"That girl is in trouble," Sensei muttered to himself as he returned to the Inn.

Since Denis Lattimore was dejected when he answered the call of Miss Pattyanne Pastor, she immediately announced that she wanted to give him good news. "The phone," she said breathlessly, "has suddenly started to ring off the hook. People can't wait to be put on Tara's Good Character witness list."

"Movement!" he shouted to Sensei. "Finally, we have movement in our direction!" He headed for his office in Columbia.

Jack and Groff passed him on the highway as they returned to Madisonville. By the time they approached the Inn, Sensei, George, and Beryl were sitting in the dining room drinking "sweet" tea.

George had written on a pad, "I need to talk... but not here."

The Inn's entrance door opened and Jack and Groff rushed in to get out of the rain that had just started to fall.

"I'm famished," Groff said. "What's on the menu?"

George stood up. "We need to talk. Let's drive up to our old parking place."

At the parking place, George said simply, "I interviewed Tara today and she lied from start to finish. What do we do about it?"

"Is that fact or opinion?" Groff asked. "We heard a little history today about the trouble the Madisons had caused the Doyles."

"Tell us what you heard," Beryl said, putting her hand on George's arm to let him know that she was merely delaying his account.

Taking turns, and filling in overlooked details, Jack and Groff reviewed the problems that Morley Madison had caused back in the late sixties and early seventies.

"And we saw the old Doyle house," Groff said. "It had been renovated. But it was a nice place. Stone. I was surprised."

"Let's drive back to the Inn," Beryl said, "and drop you two off. You can have dinner and forget the case for a while. You're tired, and George, Sensei, and I need to talk. Just remember that Tara is lying. We are not getting the real story."

Beryl dropped them off and then returned to the parking place. She got out her phone and called Lionel Eckersley. As soon as he answered, she put the call on speaker. "We're having an ethical dilemma," she said. "George interviewed Tara Doyle and the girl is lying. He is 100% certain of it. The boys heard the story of some rather awful history about what the first Morley Madison did to Brendan Doyle and his family. He screwed them out of the property that is now called Madisonville. If it's true, I wouldn't blame her for poisoning them. The others, of course, are another story."

"Give me the details," Lionel said, and Beryl repeated the story as Groff and Jack had related it.

Lionel considered the problem. "I'll call Denis Lattimore now and ask him if he wants me to determine just how true the story is that the boys heard in town. He may not want it locally known that he's checking into it. Do you have a formal description of the land?"

"No. I could go into Columbia and consult the recorder's office."

"Let me do that from up here," Lionel said. "You stay put at the Madison Inn. After I talk to Denis I can call some old associates of mine in Spartanburg. They have connections in the capital and will get me all the relevant documents from back then in the late sixties, early seventies - copies of the liens, the balloon payment, all the documents that Brendan signed and then, later, his widow. If Lattimore wants them, I'll have them hand delivered to you at the Inn. Just don't do anything without consulting him first. The weak link in this concatenation is that Walter fellow. Tell Denis that he needs to be investigated. Is somebody paying him off?"

"He's driving a new Mercedes," Sensei replied. "I didn't get the license number. It probably belongs to the family. I've heard that the Madison kids don't have the funds to pay him or the other servants. He's staying at the Marina. I'll go back and get the number."

"Good," Lionel said. "Get me the number and I'll run the plates. It's better if I do it. Try not to ruffle anybody's feathers down there."

They drove to the Marina and parked in the lot beside a new Mercedes. "This," said Sensei, "is the car I saw him enter." George photographed the car and license plate, calling out the number so that Beryl could record it in her notebook.

"Let me have a shot at him," she said. She got out of the SUV and entered the Marina Club. At the desk she affected the look of a helpless woman. "I'm Beryl Tilson," she said. "I wonder if I'm in the correct place. Does Walter La Maire live here?"

"Yes, he's a temporary resident. Do you want to speak with him?"

"If I may... Thank you."

The clerk called a room and asked Beryl to wait in a sitting room on the side of the entrance. "Make yourself comfortable. He'll be down in a minute."

Beryl smiled in appreciation and in another moment Walter appeared in the doorway. "You wanted to see me?"

Beryl stood up, deferring to non-existent rank. "I'm Beryl Tilson. I'm working on the Doyle case." She shook hands with him and then put an extremely concerned look on her face. "Mr. La Maire, I know this has been an ordeal for you. Nobody thinks about the effect a tragedy like this has on those who escape or survive it. I've been in your shoes. I know how it feels. Would you mind sitting with me for a minute so that I can bring you up to date on what my associates are doing?"

Walter sighed. "Sure, let's get it over with. Some other guy accosted me outside in the parking lot this afternoon."

"I won't lie to you. He works for us and he's been reprimanded for getting out of line. The questions we have are so simple that nobody needs to start threatening others about them. But first, I don't know if you're aware of our other operatives, two young men, your age, Jack Tilson who happens to be my son, and Groff Eckersley, his friend, who is a law student in Philadelphia. They were in Columbia today, talking to Dr. Haloran."

"She's the head of women's athletics."

"So they told me. She has evidently spearheaded a drive to obtain character witnesses for Tara Doyle. Dozens of people have registered to testify for Tara. Denis Lattimore is quite overwhelmed by the support she's getting at school."

"She's well liked at school."

"But you haven't appeared on either the Prosecution's witness list or on Denis Lattimore's list. Did you intend to testify?"

"I haven't made my mind up. I told them I didn't know anything."

"Can I ask you this? Did you ask Tara to work in the kitchen for the party, or did she somehow learn about it and ask you?"

"It was like this. She and I talk a lot and I mentioned the dinner party. She always needs money. It's so long ago that I can't honestly say whether I said that we were looking for help or whether she said, 'If you're looking for help.' It was embedded in a whole conversation. We were eating lunch together in the student union building."

"Had she ever worked for Mrs. Madison before?"

"She had been to the house before. The cook had baked cookies for some fund raising thing the women's athletic department had. Tara came and picked them up. She and a friend of hers, Nancy, both play basketball. But that's all I remember. She might have come by when I wasn't home. It isn't like Mrs. Madison would make a point of telling me who had called on her when I wasn't home. I'm just a glorified houseboy."

"Tara seems to have many admirers at school. Are there detractors?"

"Everybody I know likes her, except the Madison kids. They're technically my employers now so I shouldn't bad-mouth them. The two families have a bad history."

"Was Mrs. Madison rude or cruel in any way to Tara when she showed up for work that day?"

"Not that I heard. The cook said something. Tara seemed to brush it off."

"That was a lot of walking to do after she got off the bus. You just can't get off the bus and hop onto the Madison's doorstep. Knowing that she had a possibly injured ankle, didn't anyone at the House offer to drive down to meet her at the bus stop? The bus arrives on a schedule."

"I didn't know about the crutches. I figured she was late because of the game and the rain. If I had known she was on crutches, I'd have gone and got her."

Beryl changed the topic. "Why didn't you eat any of the steak pie?"

"I'm a Buddhist, a Zen Buddhist. We don't eat meat."

"I'm a Zen Buddhist vegetarian, too. Makes you feel lucky that you can keep the faith."

"I'll say. I could be dead now."

"What did Tara give as an excuse for leaving early?"

"She said her foot was beginning to hurt bad. 'Throb,' she said. I got her some aspirin. But she wanted to get back to put ice on it. She's lucky it hurt or maybe she'd be dead, too."

"I understand that she asked you to cover for her in cleaning up after dinner."

"Yes, she said she'd pay me twenty dollars to do her part of the kitchen clean up."

"Did she pay you?"

"No. She didn't get paid and I haven't gotten paid, either."

"Tell me, Walter, what's your gut feeling about this?"

"Her glasses were wet and she was crying. She normally wears contact lenses so I was surprised to see her show up in glasses. She was crying, but she was also peeling those small onions. They say 'scallions,' but they were onions. Little onions."

"Were they hollering at her?"

"Aside from hearing the cook express her displeasure at Tara's being late, I didn't hear much. I had to make sure the parking area was spotless, check the wine, attend to the floral centerpiece."

"Are you driving one of the family cars?"

"Yeah. I moved the car that night so that there would be plenty of room to park the limos in front of the house. I parked the Mercedes at the Modern House so it wasn't included in the crime scene. Until somebody tells me to give it back, I'll just keep using it. I get called to come to the police station to talk to the prosecutor and answer all sorts of questions. I feel justified in using their car. But I still haven't gotten paid."

"What did you hear when you went back into the kitchen?"

"Look, I don't want to lose the month's pay I've got coming to me. I ought to get severance pay, too."

"The state has a wage and hour board. The decision to pay you isn't Morley and Mariah's. The state will see to it that you're paid. What did Mrs. Madison say?"

"She said, 'Garbage in, garbage out. If you breed trash with trash, you get trash, a long line of trash. I blame myself for feeling sorry for her.'"

"That wasn't very nice. The guests arrived at six. And dinner was at–?"

"Seven o'clock. Mrs. Madison made Tara wear a black dress and a fancy apron and a funny lacy headband. Then she sent Tara to help them clean off their feet. They had gotten mud on their shoes. So she made me lay a fire in the sitting room so that they could hang their coats on a rolling rack that I put in there and air could circulate around the coats. But Tara had to use a blow dryer, the kind you use for your hair, to dry the shoes of the ladies. The men just hung up their coats on the rack and went to the bar."

"What time did you start to serve dinner?"

"At seven. But first they served cocktails and Mrs. M. took pictures with her cellphone. She made sure she got pics of Tara in that goofy uniform. She served the drinks. Then they went into dinner and started with a salad and turtle soup. I served the salad and also carried in the soup tureen. I cleared the dishes when each course was finished. By seven-thirty the pies were served. Six pies were put on the table. Two pies were in the kitchen."

"Was Tara still there?"

"Yes. She was still wearing that funny uniform as I went to get the last of the pies."

"When did the cook learn that Tara was leaving?"

"I don't know. The cook and her assistant were eating the pies when I came back to get a fresh pitcher of water. Tara was gone."

"She left quickly."

"Yes, it was quick. I guess as soon as I left the room with the last pies and they began to eat, they must have said something to her to make her leave immediately, considering she had to change clothes."

"Did you ever discuss with Tara what the menu would be that night?"

"Ahh, yes. The topic came up. Tara said in a joking way, 'What are they serving? *Duck a l'orange?*' There's a lot of ducks on the lake. I told her that the cook was making steak and vegetables in a pie crust with mushroom sauce. I said she'd probably have to pick the mushrooms."

"Is she known to be a big mushroom eater?"

"She eats them, but she's not a fanatic."

"Can you think of anything unusual or quirky that might shed some light on this night?"

"I've asked myself why the cook and her helper didn't notice that the mushrooms were Amanita *phalloides*. When you cut them up you can still see the ring around the stem, and the funny way the gills intersect with the cap. Tara's eyes may have been blurred by tears from onions or hurt feelings, but theirs weren't. Why didn't they see something? Most of those mushrooms are so deadly white. You'd make sure."

"Was Tara wearing latex gloves?"

"No. Come to think of it, No! I suppose if she thought she was handling Death Caps she'd have put gloves on."

"I can see why you're reluctant to come forward. Like me, you've got more questions than answers. By the way, that man who offended you in the parking lot is actually my Zen priest. He's a karate master, too."

"Oh. I should have been more polite. But I wanted the spies around here to think that I was on the Madisons' side. I belong to a sangha in Columbia. And about questions and answers, what is it that the Universalist Unitarians say?"

Laughing in unison, Beryl and Walter simultaneously said, "'We have questions for all your answers!'"

Beryl thanked him and said she didn't plan to be in town long; but she did expect to see him again, soon.

"Did you know the trial's been moved up a day? I just got a call. They're going to pick a jury tomorrow. The trial will probably start on Thursday."

Beryl was surprised. "I had no idea! What brought this on?"

"Probably it was a way to avoid all those character witnesses. Tara is all for it. She wants the trial to be over with. 'The sooner, the better,' she says. I won't go to the jury selection. But I'll be there on Thursday morning."

Beryl thanked him for telling her. She moved towards the door.

Walter hesitated. "Let me walk you out." It was clear that he wanted to tell her something in private.

As they walked along the Marina's promenade, he spoke in a soft voice. "I don't know how important this is, but it might be of interest to you to know how Morley Junior and Jessica Madison obtained those mineral rights."

"Sure," Beryl replied. "I'd like to know. Denis probably knows, but just in case..."

They stopped and sat beside a fountain that squirted water from a stone fish's mouth. The shops were beginning to close for the night, ducks and herons were returning to the water, and in the parking lot someone's car alarm went off and immediately a half dozen mockingbirds began to beep in unison. "The water's pretty in moonlight," Walter said. "It turns silver."

"Yes," Beryl said. "This is a beautiful area."

"You know how in the Gold Rush days the assayer was one guy you had to be able to trust because he was the first one who could verify that your claim was valuable?"

"Yes... there are stories about crooked assayers... they'd tell a miner that his claim was worthless and the moment he went elsewhere, the assayer's partner would move onto it."

"That's sort of what happened up at Bosworth Hills. There was an old Indian legend. Once after a forest fire, there was fire that came out of a certain cleft in a rock. It lasted until there was a small earthquake. So the old guy, Jackson Peabody, who owned the mineral rights, hired a geologist who verified the methane reservoir. Peabody wanted to see if the gas could be accessed from another place because folks now lived on the site. Well, this geologist was a crook. He told Morley Junior about the gas reservoir, and Morley hired a teenaged girl who was a meth addict. They waited for Peabody to come home from his weekly poker game. He's got a few drinks in him. She flags down his car, pretending to be scared and asks him to wait with her until the road service mechanic arrives.

"He does and I guess she offers him a drink and the next thing he's naked in a motel room, smoking a crack pipe, doing all kinds of sexually interesting activities with this girl. He had used his credit card for the room.

"Peabody goes home and everything seems to be fine, until Morley runs the movie for him. Morley acts like the girl is his relative and demands the mineral rights in exchange for the video. Peabody has a big family. He sells him the rights for a nominal sum. A clerk in the recorder's office starts the rumor going that Bosworth Hills residents are in for a nasty shock about drilling. We were interested in doing a term paper on the reasons people become vulnerable to con men, so we went to Bosworth Hills. I hired a private detective to find out what was going on because as of that date nobody in that area knew about the recent sale of the mineral rights. When Morley Junior and Jessica got wind that a private detective was snooping around, I guess they figured Peabody's relatives wanted to get the deal nullified. So they quickly sold the rights to their kids Morley III and Mariah to protect them."

"I'm not surprised," Beryl said. "They really were a nasty bunch of people."

"The Second Noble Truth. Desire. Greed is desire for money. The root of all evil."

Beryl hurried back to confer with Denis Lattimore in a private phone conversation. As soon as he answered the phone she could tell that he knew about the change in trial date and was frantic about it. "They're trying to trump my character witnesses!" he complained.

"Don't worry," she said. "There's something going on and your client is somehow in control of it. I can't say what it is. By the way, Walter told me how the Madisons first got those mineral rights." She repeated the story.

"Sometimes," Lattimore said wistfully, "I wish that all these troublemaking intruders would just go home and leave this beautiful state to those of us who claim it as a birthright."

"That's a pretty dream," Beryl said. "It's a very pretty dream."

WEDNESDAY JUNE 6, 2012

At nine o'clock in the morning Beryl was at the dress shop trying to find something else for Tara that was "suitable for court" since her presence was required during jury selection.

The clerk tried to be helpful; but the selection came down to a uniform: a cotton and polyester blend wash-and-wear plain "black jacket and skirt" uniform. Beryl bought a pearl broach and single strand necklace. She also found a pastel colored print blouse that she hoped would relieve the severity, and a pair of dressy black sandals. "At least," the clerk said by way of consolation, "the uniform can be laundered easily." Beryl thanked the clerk and left for the jail.

The deputy gave the clothing to Tara and allowed Beryl to blow-dry waves into Tara's hair and to put make up on her.

Reporters had already come to town in campers and small mobile home trailers. There were no parking places to be had anywhere.

At jury selection, Lattimore complained about not receiving all the discovery information and the prosecutor assured the court that he had. He pleaded that promises to reduce the charges to second degree manslaughter had been made but had not been fulfilled, an assertion that the prosecution deemed "absurd." He filed half a dozen defense motions about changing the venue or delaying the trial and every motion was denied. He valiantly tried to drag out the *voir dire* examinations as long as possible but he succeeded only in exhausting the judge's patience. Judge Harrison pulled his glasses down onto the end of his nose and stared at Lattimore directly, eye to eye. "The trial will commence, Mr. Lattimore, at ten o'clock tomorrow morning. Do not make me have a bailiff fetch you from wherever you are if you are not here."

Chagrined, Lattimore sighed and passively began to accept candidates for jury service.

Beryl waited, and as soon as the judge announced the first break, she called Denis aside. "I've been thinking about my interview with Walter. He was so certain that it was onions, not scallions. He even specified 'little onions.' Could that be 'pearl onions?' I suppose that they intend to discredit Tara's 'crying from chopping onions' story in case she says her vision was impaired when she picked the mushrooms. Their expert witnesses will testify that scallions are much less pungent than onions and wouldn't have made her cry - so her 'crying' excuse is a lie. Tell me," she asked, "since the grocery store in town is a small convenience store that wouldn't be likely to carry pearl onions, where else would the Madisons have shopped?"

"I see where you're going with this," Lattimore said. "The logical person to ask is Walter; but I don't think we should antagonize him. First, let me go to the grocer here in town and see what I can find out." He looked at his watch. "I'll do it now."

The grocer was on Market Street, less than a block away from the courthouse. Lattimore jogged to the grocery store and approached the clerk. "Ma'am," he said, affecting a partial restoration of his old accent, "Ah wundah if you'd be kind 'nuff to help me with somthin'?"

"Why sho, hon, whatcha' be needin'?"

"Did them Madison folks git all their fresh greens heah?"

"Some. But nuthin' fancy. For fancy they went ta that market near the Lexington turnoff."

"Ah do thank ya, Ma'am. Thank ya so vera much."

Lattimore ran back to the courthouse with his cellphone to his ear. He called Pattyanne, his secretary. "Darlin', can you call the owners of the Gourmet Shop at the Lexington turnoff and ask if they'll do you a favor and look up a purchase made by the Madisons? Try February 19th. If they come up with nothin' on that date, see if you can get them to check the 20th and the 18th. We're lookin' for scallions or onions, maybe pearl onions. And get back to me immediately. Don't tell them why you want it. Just get them to fax a copy of the receipt to you. Get on this, now." He disconnected the call.

Suddenly he stopped running. He put his cellphone in his pocket and looked at himself in a store-front window. "Has it come down to this?" he asked his reflection. "Is my defense contingent on establishing that there were onions in the sauce instead of scallions?" He walked slowly to the courthouse, shaking his head and alternately mumbling self-pitying excuses and accusations of stupidity to himself.

Groff joined him in the lobby. "Do you want me to check with my grandfather about verifying the story about the original land transaction?" he asked. "Court's still in recess."

"I'd appreciate it if you would. Right now, I'm too ashamed to speak with a real lawyer."

"Easy!" Groff objected. "What are you ashamed about? You're doing the best you can under the circumstances."

"No, I'm not. I've made a fool of myself. My first case and I've been played by everybody." Lattimore looked at his client as she sat stoically at the defense table. "She's gonna go down because of my inexperience and stupidity."

Rather than have jury selection resume, the bailiff announced that there would be an early lunch break and that court would reconvene at 2 p.m.

Groff caught Jack's attention and, waving him off, he put his arm on Lattimore's shoulder. "Come on. Let's you and me go sit in the SUV and talk about this."

"It just hit me," Lattimore confided. "They play a tune and I dance to it."

"What is wrong? Everything is going according to your game plan."

"What game plan? I never had a game plan. I'm in deep trouble, here. Pay attention to my errors. Remember them and never be the willin' victim that I've been. I don't think I understood the 'adversarial system' until now."

"What errors am I supposed to remember?"

"The first error is forgettin' that this is an adversarial system. It ain't a gentlemen's club - not when you're on the opposin' team. The ADA dangled a carrot in front of me and like the ass I am I kept movin' the way he wanted me to move, tryin' to take a bite outta' that carrot. He charges 'murder one' and then to cajole me into lettin' the case be tried here, he says he'll probably be reducin' the charge to 'man one.' I'm so happy that I don't even check. I'm defendin' a gal who's charged with murderin' a pair of Madisons in the town of Madisonville. *How stupid is that?* If I had objected, the trial would be held in Columbia - where Tara's supporters live.

"My next error was not objectin' to a 'speedy trial.' When he proposed the early trial date, I didn't object because he held up another carrot. Oh, he'll probably be reducin' 'man one' to 'man two.' And a few back-slappin' gentlemen lawyers ask me how much time a bright fella like me would need to prepare a defense for an involuntary manslaughter charge. Like killin' a bunch of people was 'Oops! Did ah do that?' I expected a reduction in the 'man one' charge, but nothin' official's come down."

"I'm taking this in," Groff said. "I saw the way they moved up the trial date from Friday to Thursday. You won't have time to interview those potential character witnesses and you don't have a staff to help you. But look, no matter what errors you made, it is what it is. You need a pep talk." He called his grandfather.

Groff reached Lionel Eckersley. After a brief exchange of information, he said to Denis, "My grandfather examined the records that pertained to the original land purchase by Lieutenant Brendan Doyle in 1969. The story the girls in town gave us was accurate. Do you want him to overnight the records to you?"

"If he would be so kind."

"You tell him that. And talk to him about your problem. He'll help you deal with it." Groff asked his grandfather if he'd speak a few encouraging words to the anxious young attorney. He handed his phone to Denis and said, "I'll meet you back on the courthouse steps."

When Denis Lattimore rejoined Groff, he said simply, "It helped. He reminded me what 'reasonable doubt' meant and told me to devote my opening statement to it. I have been cleansed of timidity. I told him what an ass I was and he said that the admission was the beginning of wisdom. He assured me that he spoke from personal experience. Then we talked about Tara, how stubborn and uncommunicative she was in the midst of crisis. He laughed and told me the strangest thing. He insisted that her grandfather was the same identical way. He said that the other officers always said that Brendan Doyle had a direct line to God and he didn't let anybody tap his phone. And the men under him - who knew him best - said that he'd talk things over with The Big Guy and that they had learned to trust in the accuracy of the information he got. I'm through lettin' the prosecution roll all over me. Let's eat."

Pattyanne, Lattimore's secretary, called him in the Inn's dining room. She was jubilant. "The tide has turned!" she bubbled. "I've got three pieces of great news! First, the Madisons did not buy any scallions. They did buy *shallots*. I looked them up and they do make your eyes water! The D.A. had somebody in the shop, looking at the receipt. I'm willing to bet they don't know what shallots are and they'll say, 'Tara described the onions as 'little onions' and they'll figure they must be pearl onions and there are no pearl onions on the list!' They're dumb as a sack of spuds over there in the D.A.'s office."

Denis Lattimore's new *machismo* attitude had not fully infiltrated his self-confidence. "Won't they say that they bought the scallions at one of those farmer's roadside stands?"

"Of course they will," Pattyanne squealed triumphantly, "but why would they be buying two kinds of onions? Oh, I love it! Little onions it is. And those little onions are shallots, 'stored onions' - pungent little devils!

"Second, can you get that lady P.I. to come here and man the phones for me? Calls are coming in about character references and I don't want to trust anybody who's not on our team to answer them. I need to stop into a dress shop and also keep an appointment with the hairdresser, the one person in the universe who always knows where the bodies are buried. Two of the Madison ladies had complained about Morley and Jessica Madison's 'callous exclusion' of them; and they complained in emails and text messages, copies of which I am now told I'm welcome to pick up. Yes, the owners of both establishments are prepared to testify in court. I could be gone for several hours. Naturally, I have to get my hair colored and well, your private investigator will understand.

"And the third is the insurance angle. I'm nailing that down even as we speak!"

Lattimore thanked her and said he'd have Beryl Tilson go to his office shortly. He turned to Groff. "The bird of hope has nested in my soul. Your Grandfather reminded me of the first three rules in trial law. 'Blame the victim, find an alternate villain, and win the case in the opening statement.' I needed to be reminded."

THURSDAY, JUNE 7, 2012

Denis Lattimore approached the bench and asked Judge Harrington if it would be possible for a law student from Philadelphia to sit with him as an assistant.

"You surely don't intend for him to speak to a witness during this trial?"

"No, Your Honor, just to assist me with my files, producin' the relevant documents as needed. Things have been somewhat confusin' since the trial date was brought forward."

"Just so his voice does not appear anywhere in the record and he maintains proper decorum."

Denis nodded. "He shall be both silent and decorous, Your Honor."

Groff wore a silk shantung suit and pastel Tee shirt he had borrowed from Denis that fit him horizontally but not vertically. The chest fit perfectly, but the sleeves of the jacket ended abruptly several inches above his wrist, so that Groff had to push them farther up his arm to make the fit look intentional. The pants did not reach the tops of his shoes. Whispering, Jack explained the length to Beryl, "He's expecting a flood." The remark caused her to suppress laughter at inappropriate moments. George, who rarely joked, could see Groff only from his waist up. "He's giving us his 'Sonny Crockett' look." Neither Jack nor Groff understood the sartorial reference to *Miami Vice*.

With a relaxed and dignified carriage that usually only large amounts of inherited wealth can provide, Groff, despite all defects in attire, sat beside Denis and lent a calming assurance to the struggling attorney. The prosecutor's desk was stacked with documents, accordion pleated file holders, evidence bags, two laptop computers, and an assortment of writing instruments. The defense's desk contained only two tablets, two pens, and a book.

Beryl, her digital recorder positioned in a breast pocket where its microphone would be unobstructed, sat behind Groff; and Jack sat behind Lattimore. George sat on Beryl's left and Sensei sat on George's left.

A.D.A. Edward Korman made an opening statement that surprised Tara's team by the boldness of its insistence that they were assembled to consider vicious premeditated murder and attempted murder; that Tara had maliciously caused the deaths of four people and critically damaged the health and well being of four others. He droned on for half an hour, giving his overwrought presentation. "The People will prove that a hatred seethed through her bloodstream and that it had, drop by drop, year after year, congealed into a hard and cruel weapon of contempt."

Korman continued. "Even as she extended one hand for a paycheck, she concealed this weapon and came like a sneak thief in the night to invade a family's sanctity, its peaceful rest, to kill and maim in a vile and misbegotten desire for revenge.

"Upon whom did she take revenge?" he asked and then answered, "On innocent people her wicked glance had never before fallen upon. Tara Doyle went out into the woods on that Monday afternoon and she deliberately picked the most deadly of all poisonous mushrooms. Oh, she will tell you that her eyes were watering so much from chopping *onions* that she accidentally mistook 'poisoned' for 'safe.'" Korman's voice rose. "Her vision was blurred! Oh, those nasty onions! And what a lie that is! The fact, Ladies and Gentlemen, is that she chopped scallions, and *scallions* do not irritate the eyes. Yes, Ladies and Gentlemen, *she chopped scallions!*"

The words were supposed to lay heavy on the air like a smothering curse, but the effect was destroyed when Jack irreverently gulped a loud laugh at the absurdity of the emphasis. Beryl glared at him, and he cringed apologetically. The laugh was contagious, however, and the three private investigators struggled to choke the laughter dead.

Korman looked scornfully at the three people at the defense table who had not even cracked a smile. "She did not care how many innocent people died a wretched death. They were mere collateral damage. And she wants to blame scallions!"

Beryl heard the term and winced. Collateral damage: the one part of the scenario she could not understand.

"Was Tara Doyle in danger of eating that fatal meal?" Korman asked. "No. She saw to it that she could leave on the pretext that she had injured her ankle. She had fueled her resentment with a burning desire to kill with cold fury! Do not listen to her attempts to sugarcoat the truth with vile excuses.

"She walked her crooked path, a path distorted by malice! By revenge! By spite and hate! *Set that path straight, Ladies and Gentlemen. Set it right!*"

Denis Lattimore stood up, turned to his team, and said confidentially, but loud enough for Korman to hear, "I believe that I am angered more by his abuse of the English language than I am by the falsity of his charges." Then he turned and walked to the jury.

He shook his head and then spoke in a calm, conversational tone. "Mr. Korman is correct. Many things you'll hear today are florid or barren verbiage. You don't have to pay them much attention.

"But truth has a voice that demands to be heard; and we're all required to listen to it carefully. Tara Doyle is not guilty of murder or manslaughter in any of their degrees. She has been accused without proof, without evidence, without even common sense.

"As if the settin' were one of those 'locked room' mysteries, you'll be asked, 'Who else could have done it?' And then because her accusers do not offer you any other possibility, you're supposed to conclude, 'No one else was in the room. It must be Tara.' But this is not a 'locked room' case. On the day that the fatal meal was prepared, the kitchen was open. The doors were unlocked. You've seen your own kitchens when an important dinner's bein' prepared. There's hubbub, disorder, confusion. Many people are *known* to have passed in and out of that kitchen. And many others *could* have entered it. Were these people investigated? No.

"You'll be told that Tara deliberately put poisonous mushrooms in the sauce. And you'll be asked, 'How else? How else did they get there?' Could the poison have entered the preparation by accident? *Is it possible* that Tara picked poisonous mushrooms thinkin' that they were harmless puffballs?" He paused to let his question remain unanswered. Then he raised his voice and answered. "*No!*" as if he were dismissing his own argument. "Any *intelligent* person who goes out to pick mushrooms knows you don't make that kind of mistake. You either know to a certainty that what you put in your basket is edible, or *you don't put it in your basket!*

"I'm wonderin' why we're limitin' the medium of transmission to livin' mushrooms. You'll be told that the technical name for mushroom poisons are amatoxins, phallotoxins, and phallolysin. And the supposition will be conveyed to you that these toxins are found only out there in the woods, growing under trees. But that is not true. Concentrated Amanita toxins can be purchased in vials on the internet. Research laboratories buy them for all kinds of projects. You can buy vials of snake venom, spider venom, and all kinds of plant toxins, too. The poison need not have been added in fresh pieces of mushroom. Anyone intent upon murder need only empty a few drops of 'store-bought' amatoxins in the sauce to accomplish the task.

"And we might also note that the poison would work as well if it were added to, say, the pint of cream that the cook used for that sauce." Lattimore performed the actions on imaginary items. "Take a syringe. Draw out a little toxin from the vial. Pick up that pint carton of cream. Push that needle into it. And there you have it. Was any attempt made to examine the container of any ingredient? No. And what about the wine? Or the soup? No. Or the chocolate sauce on the ice cream. No. But I don't blame the prosecution for not spendin' any time worryin' about *how* this meal was poisoned. The big issue is *why* this meal was poisoned.

"You'll be asked, 'Why else?' You'll be told that back in the days of Viet Nam when Lyndon Baines Johnson was president, the Madisons and the Doyles had a dispute and that Tara, an *otherwise reasonable* college girl, used the occasion of a dinner party given in February of *this very* year, to exact vengeance for somethin' not done to her, but to *her ancestor,* and not done by the people upon whom she was taking vengeance, but by *their ancestor.*" He grinned and shook his head, gently mocking that theory.

Lattimore then became more animated. His voice rose and fell as he paced and stopped and gestured. "Mr. Korman will tell you that she is fiendishly clever. That means that she is both evil and intelligent. Is she evil? This courtroom is filled today with people who have journeyed here from Columbia and elsewhere to assure you that *they, who have known her long and well, know that she is good, and kind, and caring.* But he wants you to believe that she is a homicidal maniac because for her to have done what he says she did and for the reason he says she did it, well, that person would have to be a homicidal maniac.

"He says she is a clever sneak. Poison is a weapon of stealth, a weapon of secrecy. How smart do you have to be to know that when you want secretly to poison a meal with mushrooms, *it is best not to be the person who brings the mushrooms to the cook!* That's not being sneaky. That's being just plain stupid!

"But Mr. Korman is no fool. He knows that you're likely to find *that* theory a bit too far fetched. And that is why he is offerin' you another theory of the crime. Are you ready? Because Tara's employer insulted her, she got even by ruinin' the dinner and murderin' the dinner guests. I'm wonderin' if I should have pleaded the insanity defense.

"Although Mr. Korman has not looked for anyone else, he says that *there is no one else who had a motive.* Yet, he never mentioned The Big Six to you. I heard his opening statement and not once did he mention The Big Six. Is that important? *Well, let us see!*"

Lattimore spoke as if he were palpating the core of his argument. "The six people who sat down at that dinin' room table on February 20th were celebratin' the initiation of their very profitable business venture, a partnership they called, 'The Big Six.' Their business was purchasin' mineral rights and extractin' the natural gas those rights conveyed. They were celebratin' because it promised to be very profitable.

"In common practice, the deed to a house grants only title to the building and its lawns. Do you think you own the land under your house? Check your deed. Maybe you do. Don't count on it. A person whose home is in a tract of houses, a development, will likely find that the minerals - the gold, the oil, the gas, the copper - which lie in the ground under his house and lawn, *he does not own.* The owner of those minerals and the rights of entry that usually accompany the mineral rights, is somebody else, somebody who can inconvenience that home owner all he wants when he decides to extract those minerals. Most people are not aware of this legal peculiarity. Certainly, the good folks of Bosworth Hills, just down the road from here, did not know it. And what did that knowledge cost them? Oh, they paid dearly when two of The Big Six investors began to extract natural gas from underneath their houses. Those homeowners learned the bitter lessons of ignorance and greed.

He spoke intimately. "Big profits were what The Big Six members were celebratin' with filet mignon pies and champagne on the night of February 20th."

Lattimore looked at the prosecution table. He snarled. "Nobody else had a motive?" And then he repeated the question, shaking with indignation, "*Nobody else had a motive?*" He turned to the jury. "We will present incontestable evidence that other people were furious with the Madisons because they had excluded them from that very profitable business venture. In fact, they *seethed in resentment* because they had not been invited to that special dinner. And these people, some of whom were relatives of the hosts, did not live far away. They were a stone's throw from the Madison House. We will show you the letters they wrote and produce the good citizens of Columbia to whom they wrote the letters... all attestin' to their profound resentment. Were jealousy and greed - *time honored motives for murder* - ever considered motives for poisonin' that dinner? *No!*" He shook his head and shrugged. "No."

Lattimore then began to use a composer's technique of letting the music swell and then retreat, only to let it swell again even higher before it retreated, and again... and again until it culminated in a wild overwhelming crescendo.

"Who benefited from the death of any of the people who ate that meal? Not Tara...

"Who took out life insurance policies and *business partner insurance policies* on The Big Six dinner guests? Not Tara...

"Who was rich enough to have limousines and chauffeurs and valets and heirs and beneficiaries to that wealth and who just might want to hurry the inheritance along? Not Tara... She didn't stand to get a penny.

"Who hated all the members of The Big Six enough to kill them all? *And now I'm going to speak to you with the voice of Truth and I beg you to listen to me!*" He took a few deep breaths and walked back and forth, never changing the sad expression on his face.

"The issue of motive must be addressed," he said gently. "And I'm gonna ask you to bear with me. I'm not accusin' people who are sufferin'. Please don't think that. I just want you to consider the possibility that one of the victims that I'm gonna talk about decided to lay a little justice on The Big Six.

"You are bein' asked to believe that this young woman poisoned eight people over a dispute that occurred decades ago."

Lattimore then began gradually to increase his tempo, while he moved and gesticulated in precise cadence and complement to his words. Beryl could see that his rhythm was resonating with the jury. She, herself, could feel the hypnotic beat.

"Yes," he said, "that dinner was a special dinner. Those six diners were congratulatin' themselves for havin' found a way to get rich, or rather, to get richer. Nuthin' wrong with that! It's free enterprise."

Lattimore paused to shift rhetorical gears. George sensed that he was beginning the 'cruising' part of his argument. He nudged Beryl who hummed, "Um, hm!" in agreement.

Lattimore began wistfully, "But I think that if I were a homeowner in Bosworth Hills and woke up a few months ago to find that The Big Six partners had hired a drillin' company to put a chain link fence around the town park - where I had promised my son he could play baseball, and I had promised my daughter she could learn to square dance - that park... my town park... that was supposed to be for sports and picnics, part of the reason I *bought* that house in Bosworth Hills, and one mornin' I woke up to find that *my family and my neighbors were no longer allowed to set foot in that park because it was being used as the drillin' site for a gas pipeline,* well, I'd be a little ashamed by what is going on here today.

"I'd be discomfited to hear that the people of South Carolina were chargin' an otherwise reasonable girl with havin' poisoned *all* The Big Six members because she sought some idiotic revenge against two of them over a vague historical grievance, whilst I–" now Lattimore's voice began to swell with rage and indignation, "*whilst I–*" he began to rail and hammer the air with his fists, "*who had an enormous grievance against them all, did nothing!*" A slight weeping edge entered his voice as he shouted. "And my grievance wasn't about something in the past. *It was about a disaster that was embroiling me each day and night of my life!*

"I, as an owner of a new home in Bosworth Hills, would know that The Big Six were the slick operators who, at that very moment, *were destroyin' our decent little town by Lake Murray–*" Lattimore's voice then began to pound the air with fateful syllables, "*–by* pollutin' our air with methane overflow; *by* keepin' us awake with the constant clangin' of pumps and pipes; *by* takin' our tree-lined streets and fillin' 'em with dump trucks and tankers;" his voice became thunderous, "*by* fillin' our street corners with grubby, out-of-work men who trash talked our women and threatened our kids; *and by* condemnin' us all to pay mortgages for years to come on houses that because of Big Six greed are now *worth a fraction of what we just paid for them!*"

His chest heaved and he trembled as his voice became a humble weepy confession. He pointed at Korman, "Hearin' this man say that nobody else had the slightest motive for poisonin' the celebration dinner of those six–" he searched for words that were permissible to use, "–cruel and greedy people," his voice became a maudlin whisper, "I would wonder what you thought of me. How could you think that she was bold enough to risk everythin' for some old and pointless argument," now he wailed at the jury, "but that I, *who lost everything I had hoped, and prayed, and saved for, had no cause that was even worthy of suspicion, that I was too stupid or too impotent to strike back at the people who had destroyed my very way of life?*" He suddenly wilted, shook his head, and with a tear spilling from his eye, he looked at Korman and asked, "No motive?"

Lattimore assumed a conversational tone when he turned again to the jury. "And oh, The Big Six had plans! Bosworth Hills was only their *current* victim. They had targeted other towns, other homeowners who did not own the mineral rights to their property. And the folks who were targeted? I guess they are as helpless and spineless as the folks from Bosworth Hills, the folks that Mr. Korman thinks had no motive at all to harm a single hair on the heads of those... heartless... carpet baggers.

"But oh," he whispered, "don't call attention to that gas extraction scheme. It isn't good for business." He looked at the jury as he shook his finger, pointing at Korman. "Take this campaign contribution and charge the girl! Get it over with!

"I know that you will not throw this girl's life away to grant somebody's cynical wishes. *Nobody, not even Mr. Korman, can prove a lie to be true!*

"Thank you, Ladies and Gentlemen. Thank you." He took out his handkerchief and wiped his eye.

A few people in the audience began to applaud. As the remainder joined in, the judge gaveled everyone to order. Groff watched the jury. As Lattimore had continued to speak, each member's expression began to register accord. At the end of the statement, they viewed Korman with disgust, Lattimore with respect, and Tara with sympathy. As Lattimore returned to the desk, Groff whispered, "Damn! That was a regular Saint Crispin's Day call to battle."

Lattimore looked at him and feigned humility. "Sir! That is an inordinately fine compliment!" Then he whispered, "My wonderful mother told me that if I wanted to do well representin' people who just might be guilty, I needed to study actin'. I thank God I listened to that good woman."

"I recorded your opening remarks," Beryl said. "You can load it into your iPhone and play it for her."

The rest of the morning was spent verifying that four people were dead and four grievously injured by the presence of mushroom toxins which were all, singly or in combination, deadly. Lattimore allowed the medical recordings of death and injury to be recited without contest, except gratuitously to announce that he had checked with the attorneys of the four survivors and they wished to convey to this court that as part of their daily vitamin and mineral supplements they took milk thistle or *Silybum marianum*, a detoxifying herb. Their physicians credit that common plant with having saved their lives. I just thought I'd pass that along." ADA Korman did not dare to object since, essentially, the plaintiffs' attorneys were on his side of the issue.

Tara's academic record was presented. She had received high grades in classes in botany which emphasized local flora and in psychology in a class that considered the tendency of females to resort to poison. He repeatedly said, "No questions." Once, he added, "Facts are facts and that's what we're here to consider."

At lunch, the team - minus the defendant who ate in the jail - huddled together to discuss questions that should be asked, and answers that should be challenged.

While they had their lunch, a messenger on a motorcycle arrived from Columbia with an envelope for Denis. It contained telephone records of an unlisted Madison House land line. Jack and Sensei quickly began the task of identifying the caller with Beryl's 'reverse directory.'

At two o'clock the bailiff called the court to order and Judge Harrington took the bench.

Korman called Dr. Wyorick, a hospital intern, to testify. He asked the doctor if he had heard the cook's deathbed utterance. The doctor replied affirmatively, and Korman asked if any reference to Tara's motives had been made. Wyorick repeated the cook's assertion that she had heard Tara vow to get even with all of them. The jury registered alarm. Korman thanked him and said, "Your witness," to Lattimore.

Denis Lattimore stood, appearing to be surprised. "Dr. Wyorick, is that the only desire the cook accused Miss Doyle of having?"

"No," Wyorick said. "She said she also knew that Tara had made it rain so that she could get sympathy. She said that she had been suspicious of the mushrooms all along because Tara didn't want her to see them. Then Tara diverted the cook's attention so that she could add the chopped mushrooms to the sauce and stir them in before she, the cook, could examine them."

"Did the cook actually admit that she let a schoolgirl add ingredients and stir the all-important sauce?"

"Yes, but by then she was delirious. She said she wanted to get the cooking done quickly so that she could start spring training with the Chicago Cubs." He said this so seriously that it seemed almost a possibility. No one laughed.

"Earlier, did you question her about her own experience with the poison?"

Korman objected saying that he had not covered this in his examination. But Lattimore asked the judge if the term "deathbed" did not include just a hint of sickness. The judge agreed that it did and Lattimore was allowed to continue.

"Yes," the doctor answered. "I questioned her about it."

"How soon after dinner did she experience distress?"

"She said that she ate at seven o'clock and started to get sick at one or two o'clock in the morning."

"What time was she admitted to the hospital?"

"At 5 a.m."

"That's three or four hours. Did she say what she had done during that time?"

"She took bicarbonate of soda and gave herself an enema."

"A professional cook surely knows about the dangers of mushroom poisoning. Did she tell you that she thought bicarbonate of soda was an antidote to Amanita *phalloides* poisoning?"

"*Nobody* who thinks he's been poisoned with those mushrooms thinks that."

"You testified that she told you that she suspected from the start that the mushrooms were poisonous. Did she say that she warned her employer?"

"She didn't claim to have warned anybody. And I only know that regardless of what she suspected, she did eat the poisoned food and tried to treat herself for indigestion. That's a fact."

"Finally, Doctor, how would you characterize her state of mind when she made that deathbed utterance?"

"She was talking crazy. One minute it was baseball and spring training and the next minute it was the scullery maid doing magic spells and witchcraft in the kitchen. She was not rational."

Lattimore turned to Korman and mouthed, "Have you no shame?" He thanked the doctor and returned to the defendant's table.

Korman, unexpectedly, called Henry Gulbis, Jessica Madison's brother, to the stand.

Gulbis had called the ambulance that took his sister and her husband to the hospital in Durbin. After reviewing the events of the early morning hours of February 21st, Korman announced that he wanted to discuss the menu of the fatal dinner.

"Did Mrs. Madison tell you what she planned to serve at the dinner party?"

"Yes."

"Did you accompany her to the store to purchase the foods that were to be served?"

"Yes."

"Where was that?"

"The Gourmet Shop to buy the ingredients for the Caesar's salad, the filet mignon pie, and the dessert."

"Do you recall scallions being one of the purchased food items?"

"Yes."

Korman picked up a copy of a Gourmet Shop's receipt and asked that it be admitted into evidence. He gave the document to the witness. "Mr. Gulbis," he said, "would you kindly look through this receipt for the line that indicates scallions were purchased."

Gulbis did not attempt to search the receipt. "There's no scallions here because just as we were leaving I realized that I hadn't put scallions into the cart. So I went back and bought some and paid cash. I threw the receipt away. I didn't know I'd be questioned about it."

"Are little onions... little pearl onions on that receipt?"

"No, they are not. No pearl onions."

Korman had no further questions.

Lattimore seemed excessively friendly as he approached Henry Gulbis. "Are you familiar with the difference between 'fresh spring' members of the onion family such as scallions, and 'stored fall' members of the onion family?"

"No."

Lattimore picked up the book that was on the defense table and, "With the court's permission," read a brief account of the difference. "'Fresh spring' onions tend to be sweet and mild; but 'stored fall' onions tend to be pungent and filled with those volatile sulfenic acid compounds that cause the eye to water.'"

Lattimore smiled at the jury and then turned to Gulbis and raised his index finger and shook it. "The fact, Mr. Gulbis, is that you did not purchase scallions. Isn't that so? Isn't that so? You bought little onions."

"I bought scallions, I tell ya'. Paid cash for 'em."

"Do you want us to believe that you bought two kinds of onions? One that you remembered and one that you forgot and had to go back to get?"

"I bought only one kind of onion... green ones... scallions!"

"Would you be kind enough to read the sixth line of that receipt?" Lattimore asked.

Henry Gulbis adjusted his glasses and read line #6. "It says 'shallots.'"

Several jury members burst out laughing. Gulbis looked up quizzically.

Lattimore smiled. "Mr. Gulbis, perhaps you do not know what shallots are. They, Sir, are *stored fall pungent* members of the onion family." He turned to the jury. "And they are very small in size. As Tara has been saying all along, they were little onions!"

Everyone in the courtroom began to laugh or yell or even whistle an agreement with the described nature of shallots. The judge vehemently called for order.

Lattimore again shook his head and excused the witness.

Walter La Maire, the next witness, took the testimonial oath, sat down, and told the jury what he did at the Madison House.

Assistant District Attorney Korman began the questioning. "Are you acquainted with the defendant, Miss Tara Doyle?"

"Yes."

"Did you have a conversation with Miss Doyle on February 15th of this year?"

"Yes."

"Was the dinner party that the Madisons were giving on February 20th discussed?"

"Yes."

"Did Miss Doyle ask you if there could possibly be work for her at the Madison House as the owners prepared for that dinner party?"

"No. I asked her if she wanted to make some money since they needed extra help and she needed the money."

Beryl silently groaned. When she had spoken to him, he was unable to remember who had asked first.

Korman evidently had also been told that Walter could not remember. "How is it you remember the conversation differently now than you did when we first discussed it? You told me that when you told Tara about the dinner party you couldn't remember whether she asked you for work or whether you asked her if she wanted to work."

"Why would I have even bothered to tell Tara about some stupid dinner party at the Madison House if it weren't to ask her if she wanted a job, cleaning house and working in the kitchen?"

"That is not what you led me to believe."

"I didn't lead you to believe anything. You asked me a question and I answered it. We talked about the dinner party because we were looking for help and I asked her if she wanted to earn some money."

Edward Korman, distressed by the answers he had been given, questioned Walter La Maire about the time Tara was expected, the permission she had to be late, and even if he knew whether or not Tara had called. Walter did not know anything about permission and asserted that he did not screen Mrs. Madison's calls.

Korman asked, "When you went into the kitchen, did you hear any cross words directed at Tara?"

"Yes."

"What did you hear?"

"Mrs. Madison told Tara that if there was extra sauce maybe the cook would give it to her to put on the road-kill her father would be serving for dinner that night." People in the courtroom gasped at the nature of the insult.

"What else did you hear?"

Walter La Maire responded in an unemotional monotone. "Mrs. Madison said that Tara was as worthless as her father. She said, 'Garbage in, Garbage out. When you mate garbage with garbage, you get garbage.' She said that she blamed herself, 'for feeling sorry for her.' She called Tara a blind and clumsy oaf. And the cook said that Tara should count the steak pies and then she'd see that there were eight pies and only six at the dinner table which meant that two of the pies were going to be for herself - the cook - and kitchen maid, and that Tara would get no steak pie for dinner because they worked and she didn't work. And then they made a joke about her limping. 'And you? You're as useless - Hey this fits! - as a one legged man in an ass kickin' contest.' Then they laughed because that one-legged line fit with her injured foot."

A murmur of shocked disapproval rose from the audience. Even Judge Harrington's expression conveyed his disappointment that a servant would be spoken to in such a manner. He struck his gavel, but said nothing.

Korman had obviously not heard the complete litany of abusive remarks before. He brightened, thinking obviously that this strengthened his "insult" theory of motive. "Mrs. Madison and the cook were apparently displeased with Tara's performance. Perhaps they felt that she was shirking and this lackluster performance occasioned their criticism. What else did Tara do besides pick mushrooms to earn her pay?"

"Not much in the kitchen," Walter said. "She had to wear a uniform and act like a lady's maid."

Korman shrugged. "She arrived late and left early and had to act like a lady's maid. That doesn't sound like a hard day's work to me." He turned to Lattimore. "Your witness."

Lattimore stood up and shrugged with his hands held up helplessly. "Let's discuss that uniform." He looked gently at Walter. "What was it like?"

"It was goofy... black with a white apron and one of those white lace bands around her forehead."

Lattimore asked the Court's indulgence. His secretary Pattyanne took off her raincoat and stood up to reveal that she was wearing a maid's uniform. She had been wearing the lacy head band around her neck, but as she stood she pushed the band up to her forehead and walked as close to the front of the courtroom as she was allowed to go. "Is this similar to the uniform Miss Doyle was required to wear?"

"Yes. That looks just like it," Walter answered.

"For the record, Your Honor, my secretary obtained this uniform from a Halloween costume shop. It is a replica of a standard lady's maid uniform worn in the 1920s. I'd offer it into evidence, but the costume shop was adamant. They want it returned!"

The spectators laughed. Korman groaned. Lattimore continued. "Did Mrs. Madison make any comment about the propriety of this uniform?"

"No. She just laughed and took Tara's picture and said it would look good on the internet."

Tara looked down, clearly embarrassed. Everyone noticed her distress.

Lattimore probed her duties as a lady's maid and then returned to Tara's kitchen experience. "Was Miss Doyle wearin' latex gloves while she chopped the mushrooms?"

"No. Nobody wore gloves."

Lattimore quizzically asked the jury. "No gloves? Why wasn't she charged with attempted suicide?"

Everyone snickered. Judge Harrison cleared his throat and then cried, "Order!" He did not, however, warn Lattimore who promptly apologized.

"One more thing," Lattimore turned to La Maire. "With all those insults hurled at Miss Doyle isn't it possible that she just got mad enough to want to kill? I think most of us would get very mad if our employer talked to us in such a manner."

"I know I would," Walter said. "But those insults were made *after* she had already picked the mushrooms. The pies were already in the oven when they started to pick on Tara. Just one remark about being late came before. And she knew she was late."

Lattimore thanked him and triumphantly concluded his cross-examination.

Korman muttered something about the State resting and returned to his chair.

Lattimore had planned to call witnesses who would establish the depth of animosity felt by the Madisons' relatives, but the emails and text messages were already common knowledge which he had earlier averred he could prove. Timing was everything, he thought, and it was time to 'play his ace,' as he later put it, and call Tara Doyle to testify.

Groff no longer questioned anything that Denis Lattimore did. He sat there in awe of the young lawyer and wondered what surprise he'd next experience.

Tara Doyle, in her blue linen suit and white shoes and jewelry looked plain but honest. She was not a beautiful woman, but she was attractive. Her sweet, unpretentious demeanor made her instantly likable. George, Sensei and Beryl noticed immediately that she was a completely different person on the stand than she had been in the jail.

Lattimore "walked" her through La Maire's offer of work, the injury to her ankle, and the permission she received from Jessica Madison to arrive late.

Throughout the initial questioning she struck the precise note of "innocent and naive." When, for example, she related the conversation with La Maire, she looked directly at the jury members and explained, "I'm on an athletic scholarship; but it's a girl's team and we don't get any extras so I'm always short of money. Walter told me that there was a dinner party coming up in Madisonville and that the house needed some spring cleaning done beforehand and also some extra help on the night of the dinner party; and he asked if it sounded like something I was interested in doing. I said, 'Sure!' He said it would be Sunday, all day, to clean; Monday, after the game, to work in the kitchen."

Beryl's digital recorder had reached its channel capacity. She activated another channel. George was also recording Tara's testimony. He whispered, "I don't want to miss a syllable of this performance."

Tara told the court how she had been asked to chop the onions before she went outside so that the cook could get started with the sauce. She gave a logical order of events. After she returned with the mushrooms, the cook told her to put them in the colander; and while Tara went to the bathroom to clean the mud from hands, feet, and legs, and to put the uniform on, the cook rinsed the mushrooms and then Tara chopped them. At no time did she do any cooking.

For nearly half an hour she spoke in a humble, calm, and respectful voice. And then, when the initial questioning concluded and the stage was set, she gave the performance George especially wanted to see.

Discussing the insults, she said, "They made that remark about my father serving road-kill for dinner, but lots of folks eat deer that are fresh killed on the road. It was an empty insult. Besides, my dad died ten years ago."

Lattimore asked why she left early. "My ankle was hurting bad and I wanted to put ice on it. I was hungry, too, and wanted to eat." Her chin began to quiver and she twisted her handkerchief in angular turns. "We aren't allowed to eat much before a game and I hadn't eaten since the morning." She choked a little, stifling a sob and her eyes began to brim with tears. "I looked for something to eat but the cook said there wasn't anything I could have. The pies smelled so good! But then she took a pie for herself and gave a pie to her assistant and said that I didn't deserve a pie because I hadn't done any work." She wiped tears that had begun to roll down her cheeks. Her voice dropped and in a shuddering whisper she said, "So I just changed my clothes and left."

Almost in an accusatory manner Lattimore asked Tara, "Did you wear latex gloves when you handled the mushrooms?"

"No," she answered defensively. "I didn't see a reason to wear gloves! The mushrooms looked fine to me," she pleaded, gasping in staccato gulps. "The cook rinsed them in the colander. They must have looked fine to her, too." The gasps became choking sobs. "I would have eaten... one of those pies," her voice trailed off into a whine, "if they would've let me have one." She began to sob in earnest as her breath entered her chest in great heaving gulps of air.

"Thank you." Lattimore turned to Korman, "Your witness."

Judge Harrison gave Tara time to compose herself. She shuddered a few times and signaled that she was ready to continue.

Korman approached Tara with a stack of bills in his hand. "You say you called Mrs. Madison to inform her of your injury. I have here your phone records and hers. There is no call from you to her on February 20th. How do you explain that?"

For a moment she seemed bewildered. Then she suddenly realized the answer. "The druggist dialed her number on his phone and handed it to me. You'll have to get his records." She tried to be helpful. "I think I saw him sitting in the back. You can ask him."

Again, the courtroom stirred and the druggist stood up, raised his hand, and shouted, "That's right. I placed the call on my phone." Everyone turned and looked at him, and Korman looked at his team scornfully.

The judge demanded order.

Korman continued. "Did you really hurt your ankle, Miss Doyle? I am wondering why there is no record of your having attended any hospital emergency room on that evening when your ankle hurt you so bad that *you just had to leave.*"

Tara's expression crumbled into one of shame. She held her mouth closed and appeared to be gagging or suppressing the urge to vomit. She hiccoughed as tears rolled down her face. She seemed unable to speak.

Korman continued, "It was a fiction, a fiction designed to embarrass your employer and to gain sympathy for yourself. A fiction that gave you an excuse not to be put in the awkward position of declining to eat the food that you poisoned. You are quite an actress, Miss Doyle."

Lattimore objected. The judge did not ask him why he objected. "Under the circumstances," he said alluding to Tara's tears, "dial it down, Mr. Korman."

Korman repeated his question, "Why did you not seek medical attention?"

Tara continued to stifle her impulse to cry until she could no longer contain the waves that racked her body. In a great wail and choking sob she gasped, "I didn't go... to the clinic because... because... I didn't have any money! Mrs. Madison didn't pay me!" Now she wept uncontrollably. "And I spent... what money I had... on the Ace bandage and the crutches!" Again she cried hysterically.

Judge Harrison asked, "Would you like to delay your testimony?"

Tara shook her head and answered him, punctuating every few words with a chest-heaving gasp. "No! Your Honor... I need... people to under... understand... that I didn't do... what he says... I did. I feel so sor... sorry for those poor folks. But I didn't do... anything. I don't know where... the poisoned mushrooms came from. I know what Amanita *phalloides* mushrooms... look like. These were... Agaricus *bisporus*, common button mushrooms. They looked fine to me... *and to the cook!*" She gasped for breath as tears ran down her face and mucous dripped toward her mouth. Pathetically, she wiped her eyes and nose as she held up a hand, indicating that she wasn't finished her answer.

Slowly, grief and humiliation distorted every feature on her face and constricted her throat. After repeated attempts, she finally was able to say, "I wanted to go home because they were being mean to me." And then the racking breath began again, and when she tried to tell them she was hungry, the words came out in distorted syllables.

The judge again gently asked Tara if she wanted a few minutes to compose herself. She shook her head. She finally controlled herself enough to say to the judge, between shudders, "I was so ashamed. They said such mean things to me. I was hungry. I hadn't eaten. My ankle hurt me so bad!" She looked at the jury. "I am so sorry those people got sick." She doubled over in the witness box and sobbed uncontrollably. "I am... so sorry... for them, but I did not pick Amanita *phalloides* mushrooms. I know... what they look like. The cook washed them. The mushrooms... that I chopped... were fine."

Lattimore stood and said, "Your Honor, haven't we had enough?"

"Are you finished with this witness, Mr. Korman?" Judge Harrington asked.

"I am," Korman grudgingly said.

"Is the defense restin'?"

"Yes," Lattimore said as he tried to help Tara walk to the defense table.

The judge asked Lattimore and A.D.A Korman if they were ready for closing arguments.

Korman looked forlornly at the members of the jury, and in their expression he saw his political career wither and die. Each one of them seemed ready to give Tara a tissue or a hug while they looked at him with contempt. Again the judge asked him if he intended to make closing remarks. Korman threw up his hands and said that he had no intention of mixing sane remarks into the histrionic brew that was passing for testimony. "Justice," he foolishly said, "will be done, I trust, in civil court."

"Are you saying that there is no justice here in my court?"

Korman apologized.

Lattimore said that all that he needed to be affirmed had been affirmed. He did not require the addition of closing remarks.

The judge, in a staccato rush that rendered the meaning of the words irrelevant, instructed the jury in the various levels of criminal homicide; and then he asked the members to retire to consider their verdict.

The court was adjourned.

Korman packed his briefcase and, with his assistants behind him, marched out of the courtroom.

Tara stayed with the bailiff. Her defense team and the spectators headed for the Inn or the Marina's bar to await the jury's verdict.

As is customary, the jury entered the jury room and the first person who rushed into the bathroom returned to find his selfishness punished by a small stack of documents that lay on the table in front of the only chair that had not been taken. He had been "elected" foreman. After all the jury members had gone to the bathroom, a vote was taken, the foreman signed the forms, and the bailiff was summoned to tell the court that they had reached a verdict. Tara Doyle was not guilty of any of the charges.

There was the usual commotion in the courtroom. The judge told Tara she was free to go and he thanked the jury for their outstanding work. Photographers took pictures. Tara and Lattimore posed together, he was smiling, she, feeling for the victims, was not.

George turned to Beryl. "Lionel was right. If Brendan Doyle had a private line to The Almighty, so does his granddaughter. That performance was divinely inspired. That kid talked it over with some divinity or other and then killed those people 'with malice aforethought.' And we can't tap that phone line."

"I wonder," Beryl added, "how she feels about that collateral damage? I don't think she gave a rat's ass about the cook and the assistant or the Morleys; but four guests at the table? What made her feel free to kill them so casually, so justifiably in her mind?"

"Let's ask her later tonight. Lionel will want to hear the rest of the story, but I don't think we should tell Lattimore."

"God no."

Groff picked Beryl up and swung her around. "Wow," he said, "are they all this easy?"

"The par-tay's on me!" shouted Lattimore, and dozens of intended character witnesses piled into their cars and headed for his condo's pool. Groff and Jack took Nancy and Patricia with them in the SUV as they headed for the impromptu party Lattimore was giving. Beryl, George, and Sensei went to the party with Walter La Maire in the Mercedes. Tara went with Denis Lattimore and his secretary.

Somebody called ahead and as they all pulled into Lattimore's parking lot, pizza, cold cuts, and sliced bread were already spread out on several picnic tables by the pool. A keg of beer was being set up. Cases of Heineken and Coke sat immersed in ice cubes. An iPod was set into a Bose dock and music blared an invitation to listeners for blocks around. No one complained about the noise. The Madisons were not popular people.

The consensus was that the six diners probably had enough enemies between them to make the selection of the most hateful one, a daunting task.

The patio television had been turned to receive the local news. An editorial commentator began. "A minimum wage employee. An athlete hobbling on crutches. A group of profit-minded entrepreneurs." He went on to examine the surface of things and how we all should look deeper to find the reality that "lies behind the veil." He concluded, "What remains a mystery is why no other perpetrator was sought. When millions of dollars are being won and lost, why did the investigation focus on a college girl who was trying to earn a little spending money, working in the kitchen. Why are we not being told the whole story?"

Everyone cheered. Beryl, Sensei, and George applauded Tara's victory along with Groff and Jack. The festivities began in earnest when Groff, who had changed back into his jeans and shirt, pulled Dr. Haloran onto the outdoor dance floor and did a sexy version of a Latin dance with her. She played along, and when he stood behind her and pulled her to him, moving his hips suggestively, she moved hers, too, simultaneously raising her hand up to caress his face in a pretended act of adoration. Everyone repeatedly howled. Soon everyone was dancing and celebrating Lattimore's brilliant defense. Even Deputy Sheriff Pelley from the jail in Madisonville came in his squad car with its flashing lights discreetly turned off. He danced with Tara and whispered in her ear, "You were no trouble at all as a prisoner. I'm glad you got off. No hard feelin's?" She smiled and whispered back, "None at all."

George had danced with Beryl in a half-hearted attempt to keep a beat that he said he was too tired to feel. Beryl knew that what he couldn't feel was the fife and drum march of victory. Again and again he said to himself and to Beryl, "What a performance!"

Beryl transferred the digital recorder to her laptop. "I have a feeling that I'll be wanting to use this thing again."

"I hope you do," George said. "I'd like some answers, too."

The party went on. The night had accommodated the revelers with a clear sky and a nice breeze and nobody was going to let it pass without taking full advantage of the clemency. But the beer had nearly run out and the food was gone and only a few of the principals in the case remained to continue the celebration.

Groff had just opened a Heineken and thought he'd sit and drink it when Nancy deWitt pulled him up from his chair onto the dance floor. He set the bottle on the trash filled table with its furled umbrella and skewed chairs; and, half-drunk and happy, he went onto the floor. No one noticed that a hand extended from a gardenia bush beside the table and tipped a small vial of liquid into the mouth of the beer bottle. Quickly the hand withdrew into the shadows.

Groff returned from the dance floor, dropped into his chair, and pulled Nancy onto his lap.

Denis Lattimore came to the table. "I must be loaded," he said. "I could swear I saw Morley Madison 'Three' walk up the side path. But I looked and if he was there, he ain't there now."

"Maybe," Nancy said, "he's gonna go to Brazil. No extradition. We will be in Brazil's debt." Everyone laughed.

Groff finished the beer and in a few minutes, noticed that he felt different, "a little dizzy," he complained. "I'm feeling sick," he said, and began to push Nancy off his lap.

"I'm not," Jack said, jumping up to pull her onto the dance floor.

"Too much par-tay," Denis Lattimore pronounced his diagnosis. "There's ice in the kitchen. Wrap some in a towel and put it on your head. You'll feel better."

Groff got up, staggered a bit, and made his way towards the kitchen. A half hour later he had not returned. Nancy went from person to person, asking if anyone had seen him. No one had.

FRIDAY, JUNE 8, 2012

Sensei, Beryl, and George sat at the farthest corner of the pool deck waiting for an opportunity to get Tara aside to confront her. To George and Sensei, learning the truth was an academic exercise. Tara, as far as they were concerned, had gotten away with murder, literally. To Beryl, it was different. It wasn't merely a study in methods, in strategy and tactics. She felt "used." She reminded herself of all the legal palliatives. It was, of course, up to the prosecution to prove guilt; and in this case, Korman was woefully unprepared to prove what he had carelessly supposed was obvious and certain. Lattimore had bungled the case at the start, and Korman assumed that the young attorney would remain incapable of defending Tara. But why, she wondered, did he also assume that Lattimore was without resources? Brendan Doyle wasn't merely admired. According to Lionel Eckersley, there were men alive who owed their lives to him. The mysterious man who sent Denis $2000 was acknowledging that debt. Why wasn't Korman cognizant of such an emotional current? So much was under the surface, powerful and unseen, like a riptide.

"Korman," she announced, startling them, "didn't know what he was up against, but neither did we. I have the feeling that we were window dressing. Pattyanne did more than anyone to win this case. Denis had no money and she is one of those six-figures legal assistants. Go look at her purse. It's a genuine *Hermes*. Twenty-thousand dollars at least. Are we to believe that she just happened to need a job when he happened to need a secretary? I don't buy it. And how long did it take for Tara to master that acting ability? I bet it was a whole lot longer than Lattimore had a license to practice law. Why didn't anyone do a victimology study? I really wish I knew more about those other Big Six people."

"You're still hung up on the collateral damage," Sensei said.

"Hung up? If we truly believe that girl is guilty, we have to wonder why she so insouciantly killed those people. Being bound by the laws of agency to keep attorney-client confidentiality doesn't mean that we should brush aside our thoughts about the deaths. Everybody's out here dancing around but what are they celebrating?"

"Beryl," George lowered his voice, "Lattimore thinks she's innocent. Of course he's celebrating."

"And don't give too much credit to others," Sensei said. "Remember how he talked about his voice coach when we first met him and how he handled George when George wanted to discuss the case? Anybody could see then that the guy had something special going on. He may have been inexperienced at law... but he had guts and as he, himself, admitted, he wasn't a novice when it came to drama."

"Well, I intend to ask her about collateral damage. She may think she fooled us all, but I know and George knows, too - that she did what she did 'with malice aforethought.'"

"Just take notes and let me know," George said, leaning back on the long chair.

Just as he got comfortable, Denis Lattimore and Jack delivered the news that they had looked everywhere for Groff, and he was definitely missing. "I had thought I saw Morley Madison sneaking off the grounds. We've looked in my condo; neighborhood streets; parked cars; everywhere. Groff is gone."

Beryl was frantic. "When did you think you saw Morley leaving? Before or after Groff got sick?"

"Before."

"He couldn't have come to the party and just hung around. Everybody knew who he was by sight—"

"Everybody but us. We wouldn't know him from Adam," George said. "Still, it doesn't take a genius to put this together."

Deputy Pelley called Madisonville's jail to ask if there had been any activity in the area and up by the Madison's houses. The deputy on duty informed him that the place was a ghost town and that there was zero activity.

"What other property do the Madisons have?" George asked Denis. "A house, apartment, a commercial building? Where can they possibly have taken him?"

"I've got a rundown of their assets," Denis said, but he was too intoxicated and fumbled with the keys of his laptop computer.

Jack gently pushed him aside. "Tell me what to look for."

"Every property I know about is occupied," Pelley replied, "but what about Bosworth Hills? Stanfield's got a lot of equipment on the site and both an office trailer and a watchman's camper. Maybe that's where they took him! To Bosworth Hills!"

George took charge. "We'll go there," he said to Lattimore, "and you, Nancy, and Patricia can wait here in case Groff turns up down here. One final thing. Does anyone know if the Madisons have a boat on the lake?"

Tara spoke softly. "No, they haven't. They never did." Beryl looked at her and the expression on Tara's face belied her assertion that she was uninterested in their lives. It was suddenly obvious to Beryl that Tara had been watching them closely for a long time. She and Beryl looked at each other, and a probing look of acknowledgement passed between them. Neither woman had anything to drink at the party. It was as if they understood that there was still much to be told, a tale that required sobriety.

Jack had the keys to the SUV. He took Sensei, Beryl, and George as passengers. Walter drove Tara in the Mercedes. Deputy Pelley led the group with his siren blaring and emergency lights flashing as they raced to the housing tract.

At three o'clock in the morning the little convoy reached the perimeter of the park. Signs that bore the name *Stanfield Equipment and Development* were posted at the park's entrance. They could see the drilling rig, stacks of pipe, and various pieces of earth-moving equipment in their headlights. They also saw lights on in the nearby "Stanfield Field Office" house trailer that was parked beneath a hickory tree. They all turned their headlights off and, as if on cue, one of the lights inside the trailer was switched off, too. "I pictured the park bigger," Jack said, and George replied, "Denis has perhaps never been to a baseball game."

Deputy Pelley and George walked to the trailer and knocked on the door. No one answered. Pelley shouted, "Madisonville Police! Deputy Pelley here. Answer the door! We know you're in there!"

Mariah's face appeared at an opened window near the door. "Got a warrant, Deputy?"

"No, but I can get one goddamned fast. Open up. I've got reason to believe you're holding someone against his will in there. Open up!"

"You're hallucinating. Go home and sleep it off. And if you try to break into this trailer, I'll shoot ya'. Plain and simple, Deputy. You're trespassing."

An elderly man who was guarding the site got out of a camper at the side of the heavy equipment parking area. "You folks lookin' for someone?"

"The people in the trailer," Pelley snapped. "Did you see them when they got here? We're looking for a young fella' they might have brought with them."

"I heard some scuffling. They woke me up, but I didn't see anything."

Deputy Pelley returned to his car and radioed the Durbin Police Department, asking for backup. He was told that their one available cruiser was taking a domestic disturbance call, but they would dispatch it as soon as possible. He went to the trunk of his car and removed a canister of tear gas and a gas mask. "I don't know when my back-up from Durbin will arrive or what good it'll do when it does." He showed Sensei the canister and mask. "This here's a canister of CS. That's tear gas." He looked around to see if anyone objected. Again, he turned to Sensei. "Think you can climb up that tree and get over the intake fan? We'll have to warn them that if they don't come out we'll use the gas on 'em."

Sensei looked at the trailer's rotating roof fan and at a tree branch that was positioned directly above it. "Sure. I can get over the vent. I'll need the mask." He examined the canister to be sure he knew how to open it.

Pelley gave Sensei the mask. "Don't open the can until I give the signal. I'll shout loud and clear when it's time. All right, let's get in position." He called to George, "Can you stall them until Sensei gets into

Anthony Wolff

position? Knock and tell them to come out. Say that we've been patient long enough and that they should free Groff immediately or we'll put tear gas in their trailer. I don't know how legal this is, but what choice do we have?"

"At this point," George said, "who can tell legal from illegal?" He went to the trailer door and pounded on it. "Open up. Open up *now*! Don't force us to use force. We've got tear gas. Don't make us use it." He tried the door knob. It was locked.

"You can't open it even with a key," the watchman called. "They use a throw bolt on the inside."

Sensei crept around to the rear of the trailer and began to climb the tree.

"Go to hell," Morley shouted from the open window.

Wearing the gas mask, Sensei shimmied along the branch until he was over the trailer's roof. Beryl could barely see his outline in the moonlight and the pulsing shadowy light that escaped from the trailer's rotating fan.

Mariah Madison looked out the trailer window near the doorway. Someone inside the trailer spoke to her and she turned away. Then she called to the deputy, "Pelley! You've got Tara Doyle out there. She drove up with my employee inside my car. I ought to report that vehicle stolen and ask you to arrest them. But, I'll tell you what. Just send Tara up here. She's the one we want to talk to."

"Don't go," George said. "Instead of one hostage, they'll have two."

Tara called out, "I'm advised not to go in there. Tell me what you want." She and Beryl moved up to the trailer and stood beside George and the deputy.

Morley Madison III came to the window. "This isn't a request. Tara, if you don't want more blood on your hands, you'll come in here." He closed the window.

George and Beryl looked at each other quizzically. Tara caught their expression. "I'll go," she said, walking to the trailer's steps. Beryl grabbed Tara's arm, flicked on her digital recorder, and furtively put it into Tara's pocket. Tara saw it and nodded.

The door opened far enough to let Tara enter. Madison called to the others, "Back off! None of this concerns you." A brighter light went on inside the trailer.

Tara went in and closed the door. Everyone outside could hear the sound of the bolt as it slid across the jamb.

Groff sat on the floor at the far end of the trailer. He was propped up against a partition, his head slumped forward on his chest, his hands bound behind him on the other side of a pole-like foot of a partition. Tara could not tell if he was dead or alive. "I hope you haven't harmed him," she said. "I'd be very upset with you if you did. What do you want?"

"Sit down," Mariah ordered. "We need you to agree to do a few things."

"What things?" Tara asked as she sat at the built-in dining table that served as a desk.

"You need to make a few personal appearances before a few commissions. I guess it's time to give you a history lesson. Pay attention." She pulled out a document from a pile on the desk. "This is the document you signed when you created a sole-proprietorship, Adams Development. Adams was your mother's maiden name."

"I know what my mother's maiden name was. I also know that I created no such 'sole proprietorship.' You're insane," Tara said.

"Oh, Yes! Look at this! Are you trying to tell us that this isn't your signature? It was dated and notarized last January. Experts have examined it and pronounced it authentic. Look at it!"

"It's a good forgery, but still a forgery." Tara looked at several other documents that appeared to have been signed by her. "I see that you've been busy signing my name."

Mariah continued, placing another document in front of Tara. "And this is an agreement you, as Adams Development, signed with Regulus Investments who own the mineral rights to Bosworth Hills. I should explain that Morley and I were forced to create Regulus Investments and to sell our mineral rights to Regulus *before* you poisoned the dinner. You agree to pay Regulus 75% of the profits. Adams gets to keep 25%. That's more than generous."

Tara looked at the document. "And you even had it notarized. God knows what you held over that poor notary's head to get her to place her seal on it and back date it as well."

"She was cooperative," Mariah smiled. "We trust you will be cooperative, too. You have only yourself to blame. We had to protect our last remaining asset from claims that arose from your little poisoning scheme."

Tara grinned. "And you expect this childish bit of paperwork to protect something?"

Mariah removed another document. "And this one is a contract between Adams and Stanfield. It covers the actual drilling operation. You'll find them to be cooperative, too. There are many sites they want to drill in order to exploit the state's mineral resources. You made quite a nice deal with them."

"I'm just a font of nice deals. And ironic ones, too. I've managed to replace Madison Development. What did you give Groff to knock him out?"

"Forget him. He's fine. And please, Hon," Mariah cooed, "don't play the fool. You know what we're doin' here."

"Yes, I think I do. Last year your mom and dad set up and then blackmailed the owner of Bosworth Hills' mineral rights. And then, when a possible scandal about their methods threatened their ownership of those rights, they sold them to you."

"Clever? Yes. We became 'holders in due course.' Safe from financial attack."

"Really?" Tara shook her head and grinned again. "I thought that was only for purchasing debts. But what do I know? I'm not an entrepreneur. And then what? Your mom and dad negotiated with Stanfield to tap the reservoir, but they underestimated the costs involved in getting the gas to market and they had to invite investors in, and The Big Six venture was conceived. That wasn't so hard to figure out.

"And then, when The Big Six was 'spontaneously aborted' and Madison Development, of which you are an owner, was responsible for the miscarriage, you had to protect the mineral rights by backdating their sale to your new little company, Regulus Investments, who then signed with me to oversee the development of the extraction. And I... Adams Development... now replace The Big Six."

Morley laughed. "And here you are, the new middleman, the Frankenstein monster of the Adams' family."

Tara lightly applauded. "It turns out that I'm as grotesque and greedy as you and your parents and grandparents."

"Now, Bitch," Morley sneered, "we'll have a moment of truth. You couldn't wait to be hailed the hero. You were gonna be the Joan of Arc who led 'fools who sign papers without reading them' to victory over the Madisons!"

Tara looked at the documents. "But why are you telling me all this now? What is the problem that I'm supposed to solve with personal appearances?" She began to leaf through the bewildering array of grant deeds, mineral rights, royalty assignments, contracts, purchases, permit applications, insurance and safety compliance forms, sole proprietorship declarations, tax forms, environmental impact statements, and other documents she could not identify. "What's the problem with personal appearances? Did you overlook that detail when you filed these documents?"

"It takes a big person to admit mistakes," Mariah conceded. "After we picked you and got the companies up and running, we had to apply for permits. Our mom and dad would have known about the applicants having to appear in person before the regulatory commissions within ninety days of application, but they weren't around to advise us. They were dead. You killed them. So, yes, we did miscalculate. The ninety-day window of opportunity is closing fast. Do yourself a favor. If Adams Development backs out, Regulus will sign with someone else. At least now, if you stay with the project, you'll have a say in how the minerals are extracted and distributed. Another company may not be so considerate towards the people of Bosworth Hills."

"What if I don't play along?"

"You may lose a few friends - like the idiot back there," Mariah indicated Groff. "But if you play along you'll be able to write your own ticket. Maybe buy back the Doyle mansion. Meet new people and see new places. Think about it. You don't really want the truth to come out. Look on the positive side. You'll be earning a respectable living for once in your life. Adams gets 25%."

Morley walked to the window and looked out. No other police car had come. "Evidently Deputy Pelley remembers who pays his salary." He turned back to glare at Tara. "Madison Development will declare bankruptcy. And Regulus and Stanfield and Adams will prosper. Nice."

Tara got up from the table and walked back to Groff. "Undo his handcuffs."

Morley stood up. "No. We need to reach an agreement about those personal appearances. One of those regulatory commissions meets on the second Friday of the month. And that's what today is. So what you're gonna do is tell those people out there to disperse since everything is fine in here. And then Mariah will stay here with this fool, and in a few hours, you and I will drive into Columbia and request a personal appearance in accordance with our application. Then you will testify that you are, indeed, the Tara Adams Doyle who owns Adams Development, and then we'll come back here and you can take this clown back to wherever he came from."

"And if I don't agree?"

"He's gonna be your scapegoat. We'll start with his manhood. It will be an assault and battery without a bloody nose or swollen eye. Hardly believable! I figure that if we remove a few appendages he won't be inclined to run around and tell the world that he's just become a girl."

"You really are insane. Undo his handcuffs."

Morley leaned back in his chair, put his hands behind his head, and snickered. "Listen, Doyle, wind your brain around this fact. You got mad enough about an old injury caused by a Madison to go kill a whole bunch of people. Never doubt that we're mad enough about a new injury caused by a Doyle... to give you back a little pain... in kind. You've stripped us of everything. You cooperate, or you go down with us.

"And don't think you're legally out of the woods. You weren't declared innocent in court. The prosecution did not prove its case, that's all. But you killed our parents and we can file a wrongful death civil action against you. And this requires much less proof."

Mariah confronted her. "We were glad you were acquitted. It served our purpose - which is to go ahead with this project. What you don't know is that we have additional proof that you planned the poisoning. We have a witness who saw you gathering those mushrooms before the big dinner. And we know about Walter's complicity. And there are a few other bits of evidence that weren't presented. Your other victims are also free to bring a wrongful death action against you and Walter. You two are going to be eternally poor and vilified."

Tara sighed. "Funny... I don't think any of that will happen."

Morley ceased to be patient. "Oh, you'll make it happen! You'll accept the goddamned deal, if not to protect yourself, then to protect Walt and that idiot on the floor. Agree to make an appearance before the Commissioners. Tell the others outside to disperse! Tell them everything is under control!"

"Not a chance."

Morley removed a handgun from a desk drawer. "Don't underestimate me, Tara. This isn't a toy. You've cost us everything else. You're not gonna cost us this."

"No," Tara replied. "This time you lose."

The back-up police cruiser from Durbin pulled into the parking lot. Mariah looked out the window. "More cops," she said.

Morley pointed the gun at Groff. "Tell them that everything's under control here or I'll shoot the bastard and claim you accidentally shot him!"

Tara laughed. "Everybody knows I didn't have a gun on me when I came in here. You're stupid and you're crazy."

Morley fired. The bullet passed between Tara and Groff and penetrated the steel partition. "Tell them to back off!"

At the sound of the shot, Pelley yelled, "Send in the gas!" Sensei opened the canister and let the cloud of gas begin to be sucked into the trailer's intake fan.

Mariah heard Sensei on the roof. She smelled the tear gas, opened a front window and shouted, "She's got a gun on us! Don't put any more tear gas in here! She's turned on the propane! She's crazy! And don't fire or you'll blow us all to hell!"

Jack ran to the back of the trailer and disconnected the propane tank. Pelley ran to the front door and pounded on it. "Open up!" he shouted.

"She's gonna kill Eckersley!" Mariah cried. "Back off. Please back off!" She began to cough uncontrollably.

Tara shouted, "Groff's handcuffed to a partition!"

Jack looked at the heavy equipment parked nearby. A bright yellow Caterpillar D6 bulldozer stood out from the others. He raced to the dozer and saw the key still in the ignition, allowing him to drive it out of the group and positioning it until its blade paralleled the front of the trailer.

Sensei saw Jack begin to level the blade against the trailer and push it. He quickly shimmied back to the trunk of the tree, lowering himself to the ground.

Slowly, the bulldozer pushed against the trailer, shaking it under the strain of being torn off its concrete block foundation.

The floor shuddered. Morley staggered to the window. "You son of a bitch!" he shouted at Jack as he tried to open the sliding Plexiglas panel farther. The window frame was skewed, and the panel would not move. He put his gun in his belt and tried to use both hands to pull the window back far enough to get enough air in his lungs for him to make it to the locked door.

The trailer scraped and shook as it moved horizontally. A tear gas cloud was beginning to fill it. All four people inside began to cough violently.

Morley, holding onto the window frames' edges, worked his way back towards the door. Tara had gotten the window beside the door open, and could see that Morley was blindly groping his way towards the door. As she prepared to tackle him, the trailer, no longer supported on its blocks, scraped and jerked until it tipped over and fell onto its side. Morley and Tara tumbled down onto the windows that were now the floor.

Sensei easily climbed the dozer and the trailer's undercarriage, as he grabbed a crowbar that the old watchman held up to him. Still wearing his mask, he lay on the now horizontal front side windows and wedged the crowbar into a buckled window panel, forcing it out. He pulled it free and tossed it behind him as he dropped into the room.

Morley, tangled in furniture and papers, coughed and tried to wipe the burning gas from his eyes. Instinctively, he grabbed his gun; but with his arm bent and his face buried in the crook of his elbow as he tried to shield himself from the gas, the gun was pointed directly at Tara. Sensei seized his wrist and forced his hand back until he released the weapon.

Sensei picked the gun up and stuck it into his belt. He boosted Tara so that she could get her head out into the fresh air. Walter had already climbed the undercarriage and waited to help pull her free.

Sensei found Groff semi-conscious and coughing. He hung by his handcuffs, his arms stretched above his head, his knees pressed against the windows. The partition leg was no longer securely fixed to the now vertical floor. When the trailer tipped over, half of the screws that fastened the baseplate to the floor had been torn out. Sensei kick-punched the partition's base with his foot and the connection was severed. He slipped the zip tie over the stump, picked Groff up, and carried him to the escape hole. Deputy Pelley, waiting at the opening, reached down and pulled Groff into the night air. "There's a hospital in Durbin," he shouted. "He needs to be taken there. George! Help me get him in the car!"

Sensei called to the other officers who were climbing the overturned trailer, "I've got the gun that was fired. They may have other weapons. I'll give this one to Deputy Pelley. Here," he said, handing his mask to an officer, "you may need this. We're leaving now to take the hostage to the hospital."

Groff and George were already in the police cruiser. Sensei jumped into the front seat as Pelley started the engine. Before they were clear of the parking area, they could hear the other officers shout, "We've got 'em."

Morley Madison, III, and Mariah Madison were now in custody.

While George supported Groff's head, Pelley radioed ahead for the hospital to prepare to receive Groff in the Emergency Room.

At the Bosworth Hills site, Beryl shook her head with pride and patted Jack on the head. "You did good with that propane tank and bulldozer. Nice job."

Tara was still coughing and rubbing her eyes. The watchman handed her a bottle of water. She sat on the ground and put her head back. Walter carefully poured water into her eyes. "Let's get her to the hospital," he said.

George stayed with Groff as he slowly revived and was treated with eye washes and oxygen. His clothing was removed and his body was thoroughly washed. Outside the treatment room George could still smell the unmistakable odor of pepper.

At 6 a.m. the doctor came out and told George that he wanted to keep Groff for another few hours. "He had been drugged before he was gassed. As far as Miss Doyle's concerned, she's in stable condition and appears to have had less exposure to the gas. She's being released now."

A nurse approached them carrying sealed plastic bags. "Here are their clothes," she said. "Don't open the bags until you're in a well-ventilated area. The two of them have been given scrubs to wear."

Pelley had been called aside by the Durbin police chief to corroborate the story being told by Beryl, Jack, Walter, and Sensei. The police were not quite sure what to charge Mariah and Morley with and were waiting for an assistant district attorney to arrive and tell them.

George called Beryl at the station. "If they need a statement from Groff or me, we'll be here until ten or so, probably."

At 7 a.m. Groff awakened, bleary eyed but fully conscious. He looked at George. "Will somebody please tell me what the hell happened last night?"

George reviewed the activities. Groff stared ahead as if a film were being unrolled revealing events that he could remember in tiny snippets.

"You started to tell us earlier that Tara was lying," Groff said. "What the hell is going on? Is she innocent or what?"

"Lying doesn't make you guilty. There are lots of reasons why an innocent person lies. I wasn't calling her guilty when I started to tell you. I was just saying that she lied during our interview."

"It sounded to me as though you were calling her some kind of mass murderer."

George laughed. "Well... maybe I did seem a bit judgmental." George had decided that it served no purpose to assert that as far as he was concerned, Tara was guilty as charged.

"How do you know she was lying? For Christ's sake, I was in that courtroom, too. It didn't sound like a lie to me."

"She wasn't being interrogated in the courtroom. She was giving a well-rehearsed monologue. But I still didn't know what the truth was. Beryl will have to find that out when she talks to her. All I did was establish that she was lying."

"Ok. How could you tell?"

"You want me to give you a quick course on interrogating a suspect?"

"You got anything better to do?"

"All right. Let me tell you a little Zen story. A novice wanted a master to accept him as a disciple. He went to the master and knelt before him and asked to be accepted. The master says, 'I'll accept you as my student when you can tell me one word of truth. Go home and don't come back until you can utter a single word of truth.' So the novice goes home and tries to find a word that the master will consider to be truthful. Finally he settles on a word. He goes to the master and kneels down. 'What is your truthful word?' the master asks. And the novice answers, 'Buddha.' The master gets angry and shouts, 'Get out, you fool! And don't come back until you can utter a truthful word!' So the novice goes home and struggles to find a word that the master will accept. He finally decides on a word. He returns to the master, kneels, and when he's asked to say a truthful word, he says, 'Love.' Again the master throws him out and tells him not to come back until he can speak a truthful word. The novice returns home and he's frantic. Finally he decides on a word. He goes back to the master and kneels - but before he can say anything, the master suddenly kicks him hard. 'Ow!' hollers the novice. And the master says, 'Now you may stay, my son. You have finally uttered a truthful word.'

"Do you understand this story?"

Groff thought, but shook his head. "Man... I'm so whacked right now. I give up."

"You won't find pure truth in consciously considered narratives. Pure truth doesn't exist there. To one degree or another, all that you'll get are contrived, self-serving, ego-edited versions of the truth. It may approximate the truth, but it will likely be tainted. And the taints are the dangerous parts. Anything that puts a person in a good or bad light has to be edited by his ego. Whatever he tells you will be his edited version. He will omit, exaggerate, invent, or attribute his actions to a reasonable impulse or plan. He is telling you whatever he thinks will retain your good opinion of him. So remember that Zen novice. When he said 'Buddha' and 'Love' he was trying to manipulate the master into teaching him. That was his self-serving motive. When he made a spontaneous utterance, he spoke without thinking about what he was going to say, without considering how the response was going to be received. That 'ow' was untainted. It was pure."

"But suppose a person comes forward and confesses?" Groff asked.

"He's confessing in his own self-interest - even if that interest is to clear his conscience or to live up to his own ethical standards. The most reliable confessions begin with an admission of error. 'I took my eyes off the road.' Or, 'I was supposed to call him and let him know, but I got busy and I just forgot.'

"When it comes to a crime that involves planning, you'll likely get a string of self-serving excuses first."

"So, how do you know when a person is lying?"

George laughed. "There are clues. For example, a liar doesn't mimic. A truthful conversation is like a dance. Two people are in synch. One leads and the other follows. It's a kind of happy contagion. I yawn. You find yourself yawning. I scratch my head. You find yourself scratching yours. But a liar is not a dancing partner. He's an opponent. The interrogator wants to establish his guilt. The liar is trying to establish his innocence. You lean in towards him, he leans back. You nod your head up and down. He shakes his head side to side. Or he may say 'yes' but shake 'no' because, as Sensei would say, 'his Buddha Self will not be a party to the lie.' Dancing partners or those who act in concert 'put their heads together.' A liar doesn't want to do that. He thinks you're trying to suck him into your sphere of influence.

94

"Another clue is a delay in response. He may answer quickly when the questions don't endanger him. But when he's near his area of culpability, he'll start to need more time to respond. He's not aware that he's taking more time to answer, so you have to be alert. We're talking fractions of seconds here... not minutes. Watch Judge Judy. When she asks a question, she doesn't give the person the time to think of the best answer. She yells, 'Um is not an answer!'

"His posture may be extreme. A liar is usually too stiff or too relaxed. Unconsciously he's looking for a way out. So his eyes move around. This is where the expression 'shifty eyed' comes from. He's either 'scared stiff' or he's full of bravado and determined not to show his fear. So he acts extremely relaxed. He'll slouch down in his chair, or pretend to stifle a yawn, or support his head. But he's scared and if you watch his hands and feet, they're usually moving.

"A person who is determined not to tell you the story will likely fold up like an envelope and lean back. He'll say nothing. So this can be either/or. But a liar will usually give you too much detail. All sorts of irrelevant bullshit. He's rehearsed his tale of innocence and he's considered all the possible questions. 'No, I wasn't there on Saturday because I always take my mother shopping on Saturday. She has arthritis and it's difficult for her to get around. She has a car but it's an old one and she has to shift gears.' Or he will try to be witty and answer a question with what he thinks is a clever or funny remark.

"A liar usually rubs his nose or covers his mouth, and a truthful man usually rubs his chin. Don't ask me why.

"Eyes. A liar blinks twice as much as a truthful person. Also, a right-handed person will usually look to the right when he's telling the truth. If he looks to the left, he's probably lying. The same in reverse is true for left-handed people. Truth will cause him to look to the left. If he looks to the right he's probably lying.

"The biggest clues are repetition of a question, followed by a question, and evasive answers. Liars invariably repeat your question. 'Did you kill John?' 'Did I kill John?' Then they ask you, 'What possible reason would I have to kill John?' It's crazy but that's almost Gospel. Or, the evasive...

ANTHONY WOLFF

'Did you go to the movies Friday night?' 'Friday night is my night to go bowling.' Or he will stall. 'I don't understand the question.' Or he'll give you an answer that has nothing to do with your question and then he'll say he misunderstood your question. He's trying to get you to stop your interrogation by making you digress. A liar tries to interrogate the interrogator. 'Where did you get the idea that I would kill John? Who told you that?'

"If there's one thing I think your grandfather would like you to get from this it's Ronald Reagan's dictum, 'Trust but Verify.'"

"And you could see Tara was lying? She sure looked truthful to me."

"That wasn't an interrogation. That was a speech. And much of what she said on the stand could not be corroborated. She said the cook washed the mushrooms. Is the cook going to deny it? Who's around to refute the statement?"

"What about crying on the witness stand?"

"I've always admired Faye Dunaway. She's such a classy actress. I remember once a reporter put a microphone in her face as she was hurrying to go someplace. He said, 'Can you cry on camera whenever you want?' And she stopped and nailed him with a look. She said, 'I'm an actress! Of course I can!' We're told that through biofeedback techniques or yoga we can regulate our heartbeat, and we accept that. An actress can do something just as automatic as regulate her heartbeat. She learns to get her lacrimal ducts to open and let the water pour out. Once the process starts, it takes on a mind of its own, or so I'm told. They can produce tears or a runny nose and even salivate so much that they get those saliva strands in their agonized mouths. Some people can fool the most sophisticated polygraph machines. Tara gave a great performance. She must have rehearsed that grief for years. She hit all the right notes."

"So you do think she's guilty!" Groff smiled.

George playfully rubbed his nose and blinked his eyes repeatedly. "Why would I think that she's guilty? I don't have anything against her."

He concluded his recap of lie detection. "An audio tape recording of an interrogation won't show you facial expressions or posture. So be careful when you listen to a tape or read a deposition. I could see Tara's

96

eyes and what her hands were doing. And when you do a video of an interrogation, make sure you've got the camera on the subject at all times. Some interrogators are ham actors. They want to be filmed asking the dynamite question. The only purpose having the interrogator in the film is to see if there's any mimicking.

"And," George added, "remember that Zen novice. All considered statements are self-serving to some extent."

"Can you tell me all this again when I have a recorder on? I want to write it all down."

"Sure. And when we get home, I'll try to get the guys at the precinct let you watch an interrogation in progress and you can tell me what you've learned. Unless you put it to the test, you don't really know."

Beryl, Tara, Sensei, Jack, and Walter came out of the hospital lobby and stood on the sidewalk.

Walt touched Tara's elbow. "There's no reason for us to hang around. Groff's gonna be ok." He looked at the others. "We need to get some sleep."

"Ah," Beryl said, "but first I have to tie up a few loose ends with Tara."

Sensei put his arm around Walt's shoulder. "Let's go have some breakfast in the cafeteria." He nodded to Jack. "Hungry?"

"Always," Jack said. "I want to eat Hush Puppies before I go back. Maybe we can get an order 'to go' for Groff. He wants to know what they are."

"What the hell are Hush Puppies?" Sensei asked as he gently tugged on Walter's shoulder, trying to lead him to the cafeteria.

"What loose ends do you need to tie up?" Tara asked. "Can't they wait?"

"We're going home tomorrow morning. They can't wait." Beryl looked up at the tall athlete and squinted. The rising sun was behind Tara. It had just broken through the morning mist and shone through the wet tree leaves like tiny lightning flashes. "There's a park across the street. We can talk there."

They crossed the street and found a bench under a magnolia tree.

"Let's have some straight talk," Beryl began. "You poisoned those people. I don't care how justified you were or thought you were in killing the Madisons. What I'd like to know is how you so easily accepted all that collateral damage... those other people."

"Do you have a recorder in that bag?" Tara asked.

"No!" The question startled her. "You've still got my voice recorder!"

"Oh." Tara opened the brown paper bag that contained her clothing. She took the recorder from her pocket. "I guess it ran out," she said as she handed it to Beryl. "You can hear on this thing what they planned to do. In case it's not clear, Morley III and Mariah forged my name on documents that created a sole proprietorship - my company - Adams Development. My mother's maiden name was Adams. It's also my middle name. This company replaced Big Six or Madison Development.

"Mariah and Morley Three actually believed that they could forge a few documents and everything would be perfect. No problems whatsoever. A child's view of the world of commerce. The papers were backdated and notarized. They couldn't leave anything in their names because they were liable for the damages done at the dinner."

"What? What are you talking about? Adams Development?"

"It's all on the tape. Just as their parents had transferred ownership of the mineral rights to them when they feared there'd be an investigation into the way they obtained those rights, Morley III and Mariah transferred the rights to a company they secretly created. Regulus it was called.

"But the owner of the mineral rights usually doesn't deal directly with the contractor who does the drilling and extraction - in this case Stanfield. The owner of the rights uses or creates a separate company that handles all the paperwork, regulatory detail, and even the marketing of the product. Previously it was going to be The Big Six that functioned in this administrative capacity.

"So they had to create a company to replace The Big Six and that company was Adams Development. I, in their childish view, was going to pay Regulus 75% of the profits or royalties. I'm not exactly sure. Business is not my long suit. I was supposed to keep 25% for myself."

Astonished, Beryl tried to make sense of this news. "I can understand the transfer of mineral rights, but why you as the middleman? And why kidnap Groff?"

"Involving me was a stroke of genius, according to them. The Adams company would be the real reason I had investigated Bosworth Hills. I wasn't seeking justice for the common man or getting revenge against the Madisons, I was serving my own agenda - getting rich from that gas extraction. Sadly, they overlooked a small detail. The applicant must appear in person before a commission. Mommy and Daddy weren't around to help them perform their criminal acts. They couldn't hire an actress to impersonate me because I'm too well known from college sports. And any background check of my identity would reveal my fingerprints that were on file. I've worked as a coach in juvenile athletics. They had ninety days to make the personal appearance, and the time was just about up. That's why they took Groff. They knew I wouldn't yield to their threats to sue Walter and me for their parents' wrongful death. Not after the courtroom scene today. So they took Groff. They're desperate."

"Let's talk about the poisoning."

"Ok. But let's sit somewhere else. Leave your tote bag here."

Beryl looked around and saw another bench. "We can talk over there." She got up and began to walk towards the other bench as Tara followed. "What got you interested in Bosworth Hills in the first place?"

"Psychology. It began as a project Walt and I were doing in an advanced psychology class. We were considering detrimental acts from the victim's point of view. Specifically, what makes people vulnerable to Ponzi schemes and frauds? Why do they make legal but detrimental concessions as, for example, in accepting a deed that doesn't grant them certain rights of way or mineral rights? In other words, 'What sense of well being makes people so incautious that they resist reading the documents they sign?' We heard a rumor about the sale of Bosworth Hills's mineral rights, so we got right on it before the folks up there even knew." She shrugged. "When did you figure out that I was lying?"

"I didn't. George did. He spotted the lies when he interrogated you in the jail."

"I must congratulate him. I never figured that I gave so much away."

"Let's talk about your readiness to inflict all that collateral damage. Can you please explain that?"

"The others weren't exactly 'collateral damage.' Every company they owned made money by skinning people! They were 'fine print artists' who preyed upon the innocent. Always legitimate, but never honorable. The cook and the helper, maybe. Or maybe they were the kind of nasty people who could eat in front of a hungry person and say, 'Hmmm this is so good.'" She stuck her legs out straight, shifted her weight forward on the bench, and leaned back until she was almost a straight line.

The scent of jasmine wafted on a cool breeze that blew across the park. Tara closed her eyes and breathed deeply, savoring it.

"I'd like to know about that collateral damage," Beryl quietly persisted.

"All right. You helped me win my case. I owe you. Lord! You played angles that I didn't think of. Damned if I knew they bought shallots at the Gourmet Shop. That was perfect. And not wearing latex gloves! I never gave gloves a second thought. Collateral damage? Let me think. Let me think back to the original sin."

The sun had risen higher, but it had yet to clear the trees; and dappled shadows covered them and everything around them. Tara searched the distance for the starting place, the first sin.

She became inordinately calm as she continued to gaze at something in the distance. Then she began to speak in an intimate manner. It seemed to Beryl that she was whispering into an unseen person's ear. She remembered Lionel's recollection of Brendan Doyle's phone conversations with God.

Almost in a confidential whisper, she explained, "Morley Madison Senior was a coward and a thief. Education? Why bother? He could outsmart his neighbor. Fight for his country? Why risk his life? He could stay behind and prosper from the opportunities that the brave man's absence created.

"A brave man answers his country's call to duty and perhaps dies in battle and, by his loss, his family may be impoverished. They've lost his love and guidance and his income, too. He's gone, and they're shipwrecked without him. They'll survive. It might be a struggle, but they'll get through it because they can't pity themselves. They see their sacrifice as an honorable extension of his valor.

"A coward shirks his duty, and his hidden dereliction may make his family wealthy. But more, he is there to be a dad, a teacher, and a champion who will buy them good food, clothing, shelter, education, self-esteem. He's their safe harbor when a storm comes."

She sat up and looked at Beryl. Her voice changed as she began to speak to another mortal. "No one says that the family or descendants of the coward and the thief should renounce the fruits of those original sins of cowardice and theft. But the record is there, and civilized custom allows them to enjoy their wealth, just as it holds them to the respectable enjoyment of it. Isn't that so?" She waited for an answer.

Beryl quickly nodded, "Yes. I agree with that."

"I neither asked nor expected the Madisons to show me any consideration because their grandfather was responsible for so much hardship in my family. But who could have imagined that they would elevate his original sins to a tradition of evil?

"Mariah and Morley Madison were as cowardly as he was. They lived in fear that I would tell people what he had done to my grandparents, that the sordid details of their humble beginnings would be known. So they struck me preemptively, trying to damage my reputation so that they could later dismiss any claim I made by saying, 'These are the words of a jealous, spiteful liar.'

"For years they mocked me and my parents. I said nothing and my silence seemed to feed their obsession. Once, in a department store, Mariah whispered to a security guard that she saw me secrete merchandise in my purse. Two women store detectives came up to me and took me by the arms and marched me back through the store to an office and made me empty my purse. They searched me, my bra, my underpants. Then they said that they were sorry. Someone had made a mistake. But I had seen Mariah in the store. I said, 'There was no mistake. You did exactly what Mariah Madison intended you to do.' Then I looked at them with disgust. 'How easily you are manipulated.'

"For years this went on and I did nothing. I never complained or tried to get even with them. Never.

"But then one day in the park, they mocked my grandfather's place on the War Memorial. As I was walking towards the brass plaque, Mariah was standing in front of it, pointing at my grandfather's name. She yelled to Morley, 'Brendan Doyle! He didn't die in combat, did he?' And Morley shouted, 'No. His own men shot him in the back!' And they laughed and followed that up with an assortment of vicious comments. It was not enough that they profited from my grandfather's life and estate. No. They had to project their guilt upon him, to castigate the victim of that first crime." She sighed. "Now you know the original sin, the sin that caused the poisoning."

"No," Beryl said. "I don't know. I honestly don't understand."

Tara sighed deeply. "Let me explain another way. Duels have always puzzled me. Let's say that A, who is a crack shot, deliberately humiliates B. He calls B stupid, cowardly, dirty, a cuckold, and so on. B is an ordinary fellow with no special skills. Now, here is the incomprehensible part. B has to take it. He cannot get A to stop calling him names because he knows that if he challenges A, he gives A the right to name the weapon that will be used to 'satisfy honor.' And A is a crack shot! He'll choose pistols! B will lose! And don't say, 'Well, B should learn to shoot!' B might be physically unable to shoot as well as A. B might not have the extra time or money to take lessons in marksmanship. So you see, there is something fundamentally wrong. If there is to be justice, B has to be given another way."

Beryl had been staring at the ground. "I still don't see how this relates to the poisoning." She looked up to see that Tara's expression was that of an adult teacher who was gently correcting a child.

Tara, speaking with maternal patience, asked, "What should B do? Whether it is pistols or a law suit, it's the same thing. If A has superior resources and lawyers, he will win. What can B do? Should he just 'get over it' and say, 'Sticks and stones may break my bones but names will never hurt me'?"

"No," Beryl dutifully replied. "Sticks and stones can injure you, but the insults can hurt much worse."

"Exactly! But if B is an honorable person he must follow certain rules. He may not strike back for ordinary remarks. He must first differentiate between insult and injury, that is to say, between sacred and profane." She resumed her search of the horizon until her eyes slowly closed.

Beryl roused her. "And how does he decide between sacred and profane?"

"Sacred is transformative. Profane is not. Sacred is without ego. Profane is nothing but ego. Sacred lifts you into a pure state of peace and truth and love. Profane has no power to lift you above the *sturm und drang* of common existence. It's ordinary and can only lock you into a world of hate, pride, and greed.

"You can't simply say, for example, 'My religion is sacred to me,' unless you have actually experienced the transcendence that your religion offers through its spiritual regimen. People pay jingoistic lip service to entities they're usually born into. My country! My religion! My football team! It's not a bad thing; but no matter how fanatically a person is devoted to something, it's not sacred in the sense I'm using the word if the person's not exalted by it.

"But sacred doesn't have to be anything specific. It simply has to have the power to elevate you, to move you out of yourself spiritually. In short, sacred is liberating. Profane is enslaving."

Tara sighed. "I love literature," she said quietly. "I especially love Edgar Allan Poe. Do you like Poe?"

"Yes, as a matter of fact, I do."

"I particularly like a story called *The Cask of Amontillado*. Do you know it? In an act of revenge a man walls up another man down in his wine cellar. He chains a man in an alcove and then he walls-in the alcove with bricks.

"The opening line is, 'The thousand injuries of Fortunato I bore as best I could, but when he ventured upon insult, I vowed revenge.' Poe understood the difference between injury and insult. We tolerate injury. We get over it. Insult is another matter.

"My father was a loving man. Yes, he was the town drunk, an object of scorn. But he taught me something special. It's a commonplace to say that a lifetime of trust can be destroyed by a single lie or act of betrayal. My dad taught me that we ought to apply that truth another way. He would quote an old Chinese saying. 'It is better to light one little candle than to curse the darkness.' His life was a darkness, but every now and then he'd read or recite wonderful poetry to me. This was my little candle, our little candle. Other people looked at him and cursed the darkness. But I knew that his life of turmoil had been redeemed by that one small beautiful thing.

"Whenever I felt sad or deprived, I'd remember his voice, reciting poetry. And I'd enter a zone of fullness. And to my father in his dark existence, it was my grandfather's heroism that was also a bright little candle. He had a few pictures of my grandfather that he'd lovingly look at. Once he said, 'If only for one day in my life I could be like Brendan Doyle!' He'd recite, *A Shropshire Lad*... the whole poem. I'd marvel at the expression on his face when he got to the stanza, 'To skies that knit their heartstrings right, To fields that bred them brave, The saviors come not home tonight: Themselves they could not save.'

"You have to decide for yourself what constitutes injury and what constitutes insult. Injury goes with all the darkness. You respond to it as best you can. But insult you must reserve for the sacred thing, that one small candle. You must defend the light!"

"All right," Beryl said. "An individual decides what he or she considers sacred... rare... spiritually uplifting. Insults are verbal attacks made against this sacred thing. Injuries are ordinary attacks made against everything else in the individual's life." Beryl raised her eyebrows. "I can understand it. What I can't do is reconcile it with all your previous positions and the array of lies you've told. Collateral damage. That's what I asked you about. Collateral damage. So go on." She smiled gently and added, "Just keep in mind that I know that I'm sitting here with someone who murdered four people and who is trying to explain to me the difference between sacred and profane."

Tara smiled. "Ok. Your point." She stared at the sunlight that was penetrating the tops of the trees on the eastern side of the park. "When Morley and Mariah attacked my grandfather's military service, that was an insult. They didn't care that this was a sacred light in somebody's life, that it was the one powerful or even *divine* thing that, if need be, could justify a person's entire existence." She became calm again. "To me, mocking a sacred thing is an insult that requires a brick by brick revenge."

She began to speak rapidly. "Walt and I went up to Bosworth Hills before the actual drilling started. Families were barbecuing in the park and playing ball. People were laughing. They were happy because they now owned their own homes in that safe and beautiful place. They didn't realize what the owner of the mineral rights could do to their little village.

"To people like the Madisons, there is no saturation point. Their greed is infinite. Boundless. The Big Six was going to destroy those families. But what could the people do? *They were Bs and Bs have to take it.* How can B fight? With the law? No. The law was on A's side. The Bs were duped or just got so happy thinking about owning their own homes that they signed their names without understanding the document. B will lose! 'A' could have drilled a mile away on vacant property and hit that gas reservoir. But why risk it? It saved them a few dollars to drill in Bosworth Hills park. They already had the water fountain.

"How can you ruin people who will use the law to ruin you? Why, with infinite law suits. I had to bankrupt them. Law suits! Law suits by the dozen! Put them up to their asses in shame and lawyers. *Now do you see?*"

Beryl tried to follow the logic. "So you were avenging the inhabitants of Bosworth Hills? All the B people who couldn't fight City Hall? But how did that get to be *your* 'sacred light'?"

Tara sat back, surprised. "It wasn't. The Bs caught a break, that's all. I poisoned those sons of bitches because they insulted something sacred. A man who dies fighting for his country should not have to bear the insults of greedy cowards!"

"*But Morley and Mariah were not present at the dinner! You didn't poison them!*"

"Exactly!" she shouted. "*And they are gonna wish they ate ten of those goddamned pies before the law is finished with them!*"

Beryl blinked and smoothed her hair. She sat back on the bench and took a deep breath. "Oddly enough, I think I'm putting all this together."

"Yes. Yes. Yes. The town is saved. It won't become a slum. I'm hoping that things will be worked out amicably between the homeowners and Stanfield. I'm out of it now."

Beryl still had questions. "What was Walter's justification for all this?" she asked.

"Think of him as a good Samaritan. We're friends and no one should try to use one of us to hurt the other. Do not speak to me again of Walter La Maire."

Tara's tone served notice that her words shouldn't be taken lightly. Beryl changed the subject. "Did you really hurt your ankle?"

"No! But what did a druggist know? Pain is so subjective."

"When did you get the Death Caps?"

"A few days before the dinner, I went out jogging in the woods and found them. I chopped them and put them in a plastic bag. It was in my shirt pocket. When I got there Monday, I wasn't sure they'd let me stay. If they didn't, I intended to create a diversion and when everybody was out of the kitchen, I'd sneak in the back door and dump them in the sauce. But they let me stay. Tormenting me was their entertainment.

"Just for a little extra excuse, I told people that I chopped the onions before I went looking for mushrooms. I didn't. Actually, when I got back I put the mushrooms in the colander and rinsed them myself. Then I peeled and chopped the shallots and the mushrooms. I added my private supply to the pile."

"Did Denis Lattimore know how this was going to play out?"

"I gave him a few samples of my testimony and when I saw that he was convinced that I was really bawling my eyes out, I stopped crying... rather suddenly. But he never said a word. He's a pretty smart guy. Wow. What an opening statement! I'm glad my case is gonna get his career off on the right foot. And I want you to thank my grandfather's C.O., Mr. Eckersley. He saw Brendan Doyle's pure light, his egoless love, that wonderful kenosis; and without hesitation he sent you guys."

Tara searched the sky as if she thought something that she had forgotten might be written there. She remembered something. "Oh, you'll hear on the tape that they say they have someone who saw me pick the poison mushrooms. That's a lie. Nobody saw me. Any more questions?"

Beryl stared at her. "No, I don't have a single question. I'm not sure I have any answers, but I know I don't have any questions. Aside from saying that I'm still your lawyer's agent, I guess all I can say is that I'm absolutely speechless."

Tara got up. She hesitated. "There is one thing I need to ask you."

Beryl looked up warily. "Sure, anything."

"I really like the clothes you got me. Can I keep them?"

For a moment Beryl did not know how to reply. Then she smiled at the wonder of it all. "Yes, you can. They're yours. And you really do look nice in them."

They could see that the men were coming out of the hospital cafeteria. They waved and went to meet them.